ISBN-13: 9781542525008
ISBN-10: 1542525004

www.mattshawpublications.co.uk

www.facebook.com/mattshawpublications

ACKNOWLEDGEMENTS

It is rare that I send books off for extensive feedback but, with so much riding on this book (I invested heavily in paying the other authors and sorting contracts etc.) I wanted it to be absolutely perfect. I mean, that's not to say I don't want my other stories to be spot on but... Usually I am more confident with my releases.

This book is a different kind of beast to what I usually do and making sure the other authors' chapters flowed with the world I was creating, and ensuring there were no plot holes, dead-ends or silly continuity errors was a major concern but we'll cover that in the introduction. This section is just for me to say a big thank you to the following people...

Vix Kirkpatrick
Matt Hickman
Becky Narron
J.R. Park

I appreciate the time you took to read through this story, and the feedback that you gave. As an author, it is important we find people willing to tear a piece of work apart as opposed to simply email us with what they think we want to hear. Although, I won't lie, it would have been nice for you to just come back first time and say it was perfect... Certainly would have saved a lot of stress and... Oh, stop, I'm joking. Thank you - seriously - for both the valuable feedback and the support.

INTRODUCTION

This is not an anthology. It just so happens there are other authors who got involved to write guest chapters. Some authors were asked to write chapters introducing new characters to the hotel (they could write anything so long as the character ended up at the hotel) and some were asked to kill past employees of the establishment - again, anything goes.

I hadn't seen a book written in this way before - a handful of guest chapters merged into a full length novel - so I thought it would be fun to try and see if it was possible. Now the project is finished, after 8 months of continuous work, I'm pleased with the results and hope you will be too but, it wasn't an easy task.

One of the main concerns I had to worry about was obviously the continuity between what the other authors were saying about the hotel, and their characters, to ensure it matched with what I was saying.

For example, some authors used the main character Henry, in their pieces, so I had to go through and re-write chunks of their dialogue to make it sound more like the character of Henry that I was writing (for instance, one author is American so when he wrote Henry speaking, it was clearly American to my British). I knew it couldn't be left because readers would pick up on how the character seemed to change throughout the book. Then there was the other instance of authors discussing money. Some used dollars, I was using pounds... silly little things like that which would show it wasn't one seamless world but, actually, a number of different worlds created.

Now hopefully this book has been edited and beta read so many times that you won't see any of the above examples but, if you do... please do keep them to yourself... I can't take anymore... I can't... in fact...

<puts gun to head, thanks his mum for everything and squeezes the trigger>

What I will say about the project though, was that I had a blast writing it and it was great seeing what the other authors brought to the project too. Would I do another book in a similar style to this? If the story was there and warranted it then - yes - I definitely would...

CONTENTS

The Devil's Guests

MATT SHAW

* ALSO FEATURING *

Wade H. Garrett, Gary McMahon, David Moody, Wrath James White, Kealan Patrick Burke, Shane McKenzie, Jeff Strand, Ryan Harding, Sam West, Armand Rosamilia, Mark Tufo and Jasper Bark

Prologue

A HINT OF WHAT IS TO COME

Matt Shaw

Lonely Hearts
by
Matt Shaw

He smiled from ear to ear as he sat there, listening to what she had to say - hooked on every word that escaped her lips, completely lost in their private conversation. She was easily the most beautiful girl in the crowded restaurant with her long blonde hair, so clean that it seemed to shine when it caught the lights. Her eyes sparkling emerald green and so full of life. Her skin looked soft to the touch and the clothes she wore - a pretty dress which matched those eyes - was both elegant and sexy. She was a vision of pure beauty and he - Duncan Bradshaw - still couldn't believe she was sitting opposite him and, not just that, he couldn't believe that she was giving the impression of actually liking him.

'I'm sorry,' she said suddenly stopping her own conversation mid-flow, 'I'm waffling.' She took a sip of the white wine poured into her glass by a waiter only moments earlier. 'Tell me about yourself,' she said. 'Your profile didn't give a lot away.'

Duncan felt his face redden. He wasn't good at social interactions at the best of times but he was even worse when confronted by someone he deemed both intelligent and beautiful - which he believed this woman, Christie Silvers, to be.

'Job!' Christie filled the awkward pause sensing Duncan's struggle. She asked, 'What do you do for a living?'

Duncan shifted nervously in his seat. This was the fourth date he had been on in as many months. Just once he wanted one to end with the opportunity for a second meeting. The only issue being that if he told the truth, he was concerned that his lady for the evening would consider him dull and go back to the site, looking for someone more exciting. It was catch twenty-two though because he also knew that - if he lied - he would need to keep track of his stories for the second and, possibly, third date too. And what if they ended up becoming a serious couple? She'd discover the truth eventually. Duncan cleared his throat. Not tonight. She wouldn't learn the truth tonight. In his head he told himself to worry about the truth in the future but to first concentrate on *ensuring* a future.

'I'm a doctor.' He laughed awkwardly and corrected himself, 'Well, I'm a vet.' His face had barely returned to the normal colouring when his skin flushed once more. 'A doctor of animals.' The thought processes in his head being that women love animals and love men who feel the same way. A vet was the logical suggestion and certainly more impressive than telling her he worked as a postman, delivering the mail to housing estates on the edge of town.

Christie giggled at his social awkwardness. She wasn't turned off by it. If anything, she found it quite endearing.

The thought process in his head being that women love animals. By saying he was a vet - and therefore someone who *saved* animals - he would instantly appear more impressive.

On the off-chance she missed it, he drove the point home, 'I love animals.'

'I'm allergic to most but I do like them. Certainly couldn't do that job!'

'Well - yes - I guess allergies would make it somewhat tricky.'

Christie giggled again, 'Yes they would but that's not why I couldn't do it. I imagine some days would be really hard. You know, when you can't save an animal.' She shook her head, 'I couldn't do it.'

Women also love a sensitive man. A thought which prompted Duncan's reply, 'Yes, some days are definitely hard going. Those are the days you do your best and then take yourself off for a little walk afterwards.'

Conversation dried up. A conversation starter intended to make him look more endearing to her ended up taking them down the dark path of animals dying. It wasn't exactly the most cheerful of conversations for a first date and - inside - Duncan was kicking himself.

'There are good days too. Like when you help an animal give birth or you manage to cure a sick family pet... Those are good days,' Duncan tried to dig himself out of the dark hole he'd dropped himself into. He cleared his throat, 'Can we start again?'

Christie looked at him with a puzzled expression and asked, 'What do you mean?'

'Ask me what I do for a living.'

Still puzzled about what he was doing - Christie played along, 'What do you do for a living?'

'Pilot!' Duncan answered quickly. 'I'm a pilot. Yes, ma'am, I get to fly all over the world taking people on their holidays and seeing such amazing places. No bad days there and certainly no animals dying.'

Christie laughed, 'You idiot.'

She took another sip of her wine before setting her glass down again. It was nearly empty now. Between them, on the edge of the table, there was a bucket of ice with the wine bottle nestled within. Duncan pulled the half-full bottle from the bucket and poured for Christie, filling her glass once more.

'Are you trying to get me drunk?' she giggled.

For the third time that evening, Duncan's face flushed. 'No, I just thought...'

'It's okay. I'm teasing.' Christie looked around the restaurant. It was nearly full with various people sitting at the tables. They were being served by smartly dressed waiters and waitresses wearing black trousers, white shirts and little black bow ties. It was a fancy establishment for sure and one neither Duncan nor Christie had visited before.

*

As far as dates went, it had been a success in Duncan's mind. He liked Christie and - given with how she was talking to him - she seemed to like him too. Even so, he still struggled to shake off the uncomfortable butterflies flitting around in his belly and - now - they seemed to be causing more of a stir as he realised he was running out of things to say. Thinking on his feet, he followed Christie's gaze around the room and asked, 'Do you think they're on first dates too?'

'Not those two!' Christie nodded towards a middle-aged couple in the corner of the room. Neither of them were talking and both were engrossed in what was happening on their mobile phones. 'They've definitely been married for a few years. This is - I reckon - what they call *date night*. They come out once a month to try and rekindle their passion for each other.

Instead they end up sitting on their phones for the evening, or texting the friends they'd rather be hanging out with.'

Duncan laughed and nodded towards another couple in the opposite corner. He asked, 'What about those two?'

Christie didn't look. She had a question of her own, 'If we ended up going out...'

Suddenly Duncan's own question didn't seem as important as he turned his attention to where Christie was going with this line of questioning.

'What would we tell people?' she finished.

Duncan frowned. 'What do you mean?'

'How we met.' She explained a little clearer, 'What would we tell people?'

Duncan still didn't really understand what she meant. They had met online: a dating website where he had met the rest of his dates. He didn't think this was a problem and yet, the way Christie spoke, she almost sounded embarrassed by it.

'Internet?' he asked.

She shook her head. 'We can't say that.'

'We can't?'

'No.'

'But why - it's the truth...' Duncan's face flushed again when he realised how hypocritical he was being. He tried to ignore the burning sensation under his skin and the other lies that were now popping into his mind. Thankfully, Christie continued offering him enough distraction to push the sudden barrage of unwanted thoughts to one side.

'Because it's a cliché. Do you want to be known as a cliché?'

'Well - no - not really.' He paused. 'A cliché? Really?'

She nodded. 'You know, when I tell my friends I'm going on a date, I always tell them I met them out and about in everyday life. I met a man in a coffee shop and he asked for my number. I met a man in the supermarket, when he let me go in front of him in the queue. We got talking and - yep - I got his number... I met a man...'

'So you lie?' Duncan's own lies felt more forgivable knowing they were cut from the same cloth.

'I wouldn't call it a lie. I mean, that sounds a little harsh...'

Damn face flushed again.

Christie continued, 'I just - I don't know - bend the truth?'

'Also known as a lie.'

She shifted in her seat uncomfortably. Duncan knew women liked animals. He knew they liked flowers: which is why he had brought a single red rose to the date, a rose which now stuck from the top of Christie's handbag on the back of her chair. Apparently he wasn't aware they didn't like it when you implied they were liars. It was a lesson he learned very quickly though by reading her body language.

'You were going on holiday.'

'I beg your pardon?' Christie raised an eyebrow.

'You were going on holiday and I was the one who flew you there. I was doing my pre-checks when I noticed you walking towards the steps leading to the plane. Your hair was tied back in a pony-tail, you were wearing a flowing dress as you knew you'd be more comfortable in-flight and you had a single piece of carry-on. By the time you climbed the stairs and boarded the plane, I was standing there ready to greet you. It's not something I do with all of my passengers but - well - you caught my eye.'

Christie didn't say anything for a moment. She was just sitting there, looking at Duncan, impressed that he had come up with all of that so fast.

'Well that's certainly one story.' She laughed. 'You've done this before, haven't you?'

'No. You're the first passenger I dated.'

She laughed again.

'But how does that tie in with being a vet?' she asked.

'We can't use that as a meeting place. You're allergic to animals.'

And another laugh, this time interrupted by the waiter who had been serving them for the evening. 'Can I get you anything else? Tea? Coffee?'

Duncan looked at Christie. A simple gesture offering her the chance to decide for them. She noticed and turned to the waiter.

'No, thank you, can we just get the bill please?'

'Certainly.'

The waiter ventured off to print the bill out for them.

'You didn't want another drink?' Duncan asked.

'At these prices? No, thank you.' Duncan tried to hide his disappointment. He wasn't ready for the evening to come to an end. He liked this girl more than any of the other girls he had met on the site and with his track record of getting to a second date, he was worried it was over. Christie continued, 'We can get another drink somewhere else.'

The relief on Duncan's face was obvious.

'Even cheaper if we go back to your place.' Christie continued. She laughed as Duncan blushed again. 'You realise you go red very easily, right?' Duncan laughed too despite hoping she hadn't noticed. It was the curse of the *red heads* of which Duncan was one, with a thick mop of red hair. 'Anyway don't go counting your eggs before they're hatched, it doesn't mean you're onto a promise. Just, I'm having a nice time and don't want it to come to an end just yet.'

He grinned from ear to ear. 'You're having a nice time'

'Yes. Why…' Sudden panic on her face as she asked, 'Aren't you?'

'Of course I am.' The smile remained on his face - now a permanent fixture with the knowledge his date was having a good time.

She teased him, 'Then why did you ask?'

'Well - to be honest - I am surprised you're not having a *spectacular* time.' He knew better than to tell Christie that he had been worried she didn't like him. One thing he had learned over the various dates and messages sent to prospective dates was that girls were turned off when it came to a man with low self-confidence. Knowing that some girls were also turned off by a man deemed arrogant, he followed up his reply with a playful wink. The desired result was achieved and she laughed just as the bill was placed on the table between them by the returning waiter. A single detailed receipt in a blue leather wallet, very posh.

'Whenever you're ready,' he told them - not wishing to rush them.

Christie reached back for her handbag. Pulling it round so that she could reach into it, she pulled out her purse.

Duncan told her, 'You don't need that. I got this.'

'What? No. It's too much.'

'I asked you out, therefore I pay. That's how it works. I'm old-school like that.'

'I'll be angry if you don't let me pay.'

'Well - it would be a shame to end the evening with you angry.' He pulled his wallet out and opened it up revealing no cards but - instead - a wad of notes, most of which were twenties. With the way he opened the wallet, the money didn't go unnoticed by Christie. Women like men with money, right? This was another lie on Duncan's part. He didn't have money. He had debt and women didn't like men with debts as it showed they weren't in control of their finances. As for the lack of plastic? At home he had a stack of credit cards - most of which were maxed out. He counted out a couple of hundred dollars and put the money down in the open wallet which contained the bill. He closed it back up again and pushed it to the side of the table, ready for the waiter to take it away.

'So back to your place then?' Christie asked. 'My flatmate is home so we wouldn't get any peace and quiet. She'd hang around trying to get to know you, asking all sorts of inappropriate questions.'

'Sounds fun.'

Women don't like sarcasm. Duncan kicked himself.

'So where do you live?'

'Well - usually... I live on the outskirts of town. At the moment I'm in a hotel around the corner?'

'Really?! Why?'

'I'm having some work done on the place. I work in town anyway so I figured it was easier just to stay in a hotel.' It was a convincing lie and one which skirted around the fact that - actually - he lived nearby and, worse than that, his wife still lived there. Admittedly she was only his wife on paper, they hadn't been *together* for a good number of months now but that wasn't the point. Women didn't like baggage.

Christie smiled seductively, 'Well then - your hotel will have a bar I'm sure and, if not, there's always room service.'

Duncan smiled, 'Yes to both.'

He stood up and took his coat from the back of the chair. He slipped it on and waved the waiter over to collect the bill. He didn't need to wait for any change but wasn't comfortable with leaving cash on a table. Especially in such a busy restaurant.

The waiter collected the wallet up as he watched the happy couple take their leave - both of them smiling, both of them laughing. He had no idea that, by morning, they would both be dead. Only one person knew of the fate that awaited them and even he was surprised by the appearance of a second victim, not that he had a problem with killing two. To this man, a second victim was a bonus.

Filthy Movie
by
Wade H. Garrett

Duncan and Christie were hot and heavy into sex when someone knocked on the door of their hotel room.

Knock, knock, knock!

They ignored the person, deeply immersed in their carnal activity.

Knock, knock, knock!

Becoming aggravated, Duncan shouted, 'Go away! We're busy!'

Knock!

'I said go away!'

Knock, knock, knock!

Christie began to feel unsettled. 'Maybe it's important.'

'It's nothing. Probably just housekeeping.'

Knock, knock!

She pushed him from on top of her. 'I can't do this with someone out there. Go see what they want.'

Duncan grabbed a pillow to cover his modesty, then marched to the door and slung it open. 'What?'

Henry stood in the hallway, a folded tripod with a camera resting on his shoulder. 'Sorry to disturb you.'

Duncan looked back at Christie. 'It's okay. It's just the manager.' He looked at Henry. 'What's up?'

'Like I said, I'm sorry to disturb you, but we have a noise policy.'

'I didn't know we were being loud.'

Henry smiled and shook his head. 'You weren't loud enough. But I can help with that.'

'Huh?'

Henry started whistling 'Ring Around the Roses' as he walked into the room without a care in the world. His hotel, his rules.

Duncan held out one of his hands as he stepped back. 'Hold up! What are you doing?'

Henry shut and locked the door with a key pulled from his pocket. He turned back into the room, slipped the key back from where he had got it and then opened the legs on the tripod. He set it on the floor. An old school camcorder, the kind that used VCR tapes, was mounted on top of it. 'Would you two be interested in making a filthy movie?'

Duncan frowned and snapped, 'What the hell, dude? You can't just barge in here and ask us that.'

Christie sat on the bed holding a blanket across her chest. 'You need to leave!'

Henry looked at them blankly. He didn't care about their protests. If anything, he actually enjoyed it. The fact they wanted him to leave just made what was to come that much more exciting for him. 'Hell, I had to ask.'

Duncan pushed the tripod into him. 'Take your camera and get the fuck out of here!'

Henry pulled out a long, serrated knife and waved it in Duncan's face. 'I don't like your attitude, boy! I gave you shelter, somewhere to fuck your date and this is how you repay me?'

Duncan backed away with his hands raised in the air. 'Go easy, man! We don't want any trouble.'

Christie leapt to the side of the bed and quickly dug through her purse that was on the nightstand. She pulled out her mobile phone. 'I'm going to call the police if you don't leave!'

Henry smiled. 'Hmm... I guess we could turn this into a gang-bang. See if they'll send over several handsome fellas. They can fuck you while sissy boy here watches.' He nodded towards Duncan.

She attempted to dial the police, but noticed her phone didn't have reception. Even so, he didn't necessarily know that and if it meant he left the room... She pretended to speak to someone on the other end of the line, 'Yes, we're at The Grande Hotel, room 3. There's a crazy man threatening to kill me and my friend. Please send help. Yes, his name is Henry. He's the hotel manager. You have a car nearby? Please hurry.' She pretended to hang up the call.

She turned to Henry and warned him, 'The cops will be here any minute, so you better leave.'

He positioned the knife under his armpit, between body and arm, and then clapped. 'Wow! What a great actress. You're perfect for my movie.' He nodded toward Duncan. 'But I don't know about him though. He seems like a pansy.'

'You need to leave, you sick fuck!'

Duncan knew he had to regain control. He couldn't just stand there and do nothing. He also had his doubts about Henry. *Was he just trying to scare them?* In a stern voice, he pointed towards the door. 'You need to get out of here now before I kick your ass!'

The smile on Henry's face turned to a frown. His expression turning venomous. 'You little cunt! I'll fucking gut you!' He swung the blade towards him, cutting a shallow laceration in his chest.

Duncan screamed as he fell back, both from the shock and the pain. Quickly, he regained his composure and ran and grabbed a chair, holding it out in self-defense. 'You fucking stay away from us!'

Henry grabbed one of the legs and jerked it away from him, then threw it across the room. 'We can do this the easy way or hard way.'

Christie took off running for the door, but it was locked. In a panic, she started beating on it while yelling, 'Help! Someone please help us!'

Duncan felt vulnerable, standing - naked - in front of Henry with only the chair between them. Henry was just standing there, in front of him, with that fucking grin on his face and look of hate in his black eyes.

As Duncan looked around, he noticed curtains. *A window.* A way out from this nightmare. When he jerked back the curtains, his heart seemed to stop. There was no window, just brick. Duncan felt his consciousness begin to slip away as he received a blow to the back of his head from the bottom of Henry's knife. His legs unsteady, he fell to the floor.

Henry turned and glared at Christie. 'Get your ass over to the bed!'

She held her hands out as she eased across the room. 'Okay, okay! I'm doing what you ask! Please don't hurt me!'

He pointed to the mattress. 'Pull that off.'

With a hand over her mouth, she looked at Duncan. His head was lying in a pool of blood. 'Is he dead?'

'You're gonna be dead if you don't do what the fuck I say!'

'I'm doing it!' She grabbed the king-sized mattress and pulled it onto the floor, revealing a bloodstained wooden platform. She became nauseous when she noticed there were two red outlines in the shape of human bodies lying side by side on the platform. Rusted shackles were laying at each of the outlined ankles, wrists and necks. 'What is this?' She looked at him with a terrified expression. 'Please let me go! I haven't done anything to you!'

Henry pointed to the headboard with the tip of his knife. 'Open that up.'

'Why are you doing this?'

'I said open the fucking headboard!'

She was shaking with fear as she opened two doors. The inside of the headboard contained a large mirror. *This can't be happening.* It was similar to being in a snuff film. She knew deep inside the horror that lay ahead if she didn't find a way to fight back. The thought of Henry doing *anything* to her made her sick. There was no way she could overpower him, but maybe she could reason with him. She sat on her knees, a forlorn expression on her face, and said, 'You seem like a good person. If you....'

He interrupted her by laughing. 'I'd hate to see what your definition of a bad person is.' He glared at her. 'Now stop trying to patronize me and secure those shackles to your ankles.'

'Please don't do this! If you let me go, I won't say anything!'

'You swear?'

Her eyes opened wide. 'Yes. I swear I won't.'

'What about your date?'

'I don't even know him that well.'

'Aren't you just a ruthless bitch?'

'What?'

'I couldn't have picked a better actress for my movie.'

Her expression changed to a grimace of terror. 'Hold up! I thought you were going to let me go.'

'You thought wrong. Now put those shackles around your ankles before I cut off your fucking tits.' He waved the knife towards her with a menacing smile on his face.

She picked up the shackle that was lying next to the outlined right foot. Her stomach got queasy when she noticed it was attached to a cable that ran through a hole in the platform. She started having a panic attack. 'Please don't make me do this!'

He held up the knife. 'You can do as I say or I can just go right ahead and cut you - which would you prefer?'

'You're scaring me! Please don't do this! I'm begging you!' She knew once she was restrained she would be at his mercy. She needed to get someone's attention, so she ran to the far wall which she presumed separated her room from the next and started beating on it as she shouted, 'Please help me! I need help! He's going to hurt me! Help! Help! Please help me!'

Henry started banging on the wall too while yelling, 'Please help me too! Please hurry! I need help!' He started walking towards her.

She ran to the other side of the room. 'Please - let me go! Someone will be coming...'

'No they won't.'

'Someone would have heard that!'

'You can rant and rave all you want, but the room is soundproof.'

Her heart skipped a beat. 'You're lying!'

'Am I?'

'What the fuck is wrong with you? Why are you doing this to me?'

'Like you said, I'm a psycho. Now get your backside on that platform. Unless you want me to go through with my promise and cut your breasts off? I'm happy either way...' He waved the knife at her again. 'I'm not sure you will be though.'

She wasn't sure what to do. All kinds of thoughts were running through her mind. *There was no way the room was soundproof. No one would go through that much trouble. He was just trying to bluff her.* She had a strong feeling that someone had heard the commotion, so she decided to play along with his demands. She was hoping she would be rescued before the sick bastard had a chance to touch. She got on the platform. 'Okay! I'll do it! Just calm down!'

'Shackle your legs.'

Her hands were trembling as she closed the shackles around her ankles. She became nauseous when she heard the clicking sound they made as they locked into place. It felt like she had just signed her own death warrant.

Henry pointed to the shackle behind her. 'Put that one around your neck.'

'There's no need! I can't go anywhere with my legs shackled!'

'You might if they get severed.'

Her eyes widened and her pupils dilated with terror. 'What? Why would that happen?' She began to cry. 'Why are you doing this to me? I haven't done anything to you! I just want to go home!'

It would have been simple enough for Henry to restrain her himself, but sometimes he enjoyed playing cruel, mental games with his victims. He knew the anticipation of the unknown can be a very agonizing, emotional experience. Torturing a person's mind can be just as painful as the torture of the flesh. He always liked mixing the two, as he found fear enhanced the physical pain. And he had plenty of mind-games planned for Duncan and her.

She knew it wouldn't do any good to plead with this man. She just hoped someone had heard her scream for help. That was the only chance she had in being saved from this nightmare. When she picked up the shackle behind her, the cable easily came through the hole, giving her plenty of slack to reach her neck. She wondered how long the cables were. It didn't make sense they were so long if they were meant to be restraints. That provided her with little comfort.

When she was done locking the shackle to her neck, Henry had her secure her wrists too. 'See, that wasn't so bad, was it?'

'What are you going to do to me?'

'Nothing.' He dragged Duncan's unconscious body onto the platform and started securing him with the shackles.

Now she was closer to Duncan, she noticed the subtle rise and fall of his chest. 'He's alive?'

'Of course. I can't make a movie without him.' He thought for a moment. 'Well, I could, but it wouldn't be as much fun with only one actor.'

She kept telling herself that, when this was over, the sick son-of-a-bitch would pay for what he had done. The thought of him sitting behind bars for the rest of his life was the motivation she needed to get through this.

When Henry had Duncan secured, he lay on his back between the two of them. He turned on the TV with a remote, lit a cigarette, then got comfortable as he watched an old rerun of Monty Python. Christie didn't know what to think. She was sitting nude next to this psycho as he laughed at the TV. *What the fuck*. This sick bastard is acting like there is nothing wrong. She looked over at Duncan, urging him to wake up since Henry's guard was down. Between them both, they could take his knife and end this *nightmare. Especially since the idiot had too much slack in their restraints.*

A few minutes later, Duncan started coming around. Henry nudged him in the side. 'Here, take this.' He held out a half-smoked cigarette.

Duncan took it, still dazed and confused. 'What's going on?'

Henry slid off the platform. 'It's show time.' He quickly left the room.

Duncan sat up, rubbing his head. 'What happened?'

Christie started freaking out. 'We're being held hostage! Don't you remember?'

His head started clearing up. 'Oh, fuck!' He looked around, noticing they were wearing shackles. 'Why are we restrained?'

'He did this! He's crazy!'

He looked at her. 'He better not have touched you.'

'He hasn't. But we need to find a way to get out of here before he comes back.'

The cables had enough slack to allow her to help him stand up. When they got to the edge of the platform, the slack ran out. 'Oh shit!' She pulled on one of the cables as hard as she could. 'Help me!'

He started pulling on it with her. 'It's no use. It's braided cable. We're not going to be able to break it. We have to find another way.' He turned to the headboard and started banging on the wall above it. 'Help! We're being held hostage! Hey! Can anyone hear me?'

He looked back at her. 'I can't hear anyone on the other side.'

'He said the walls are soundproof. I'm not sure if he was telling the truth.'

'If the bastard went through the trouble to build this platform, then he probably did make this room soundproof.'

'I think this is some kind of studio where he makes movies.'

'Sick fuck! If I can get my hands on him, I'll...'

'What about his knife?'

'Shit, shit, shit.... This isn't good...'

Her eyes widened suddenly. 'I've got an idea! We have to get him to drop his guard.'

'How are we going to do that?'

'We'll pretend to play along with his sick game. And when he feels comfortable with us, we can both jump him.'

'You think he'll come that close?'

'He did earlier when he was lying between us.'

'But I was unconscious.'

'That's because he didn't feel threatened. That's why I think it will work.'

'Okay. But then what?'

She held up one of the cables. 'We can strangle his ass with one of these.'

'Damn, girl! I'm impressed.'

'I grew up with three brothers, so I know how to take care of myself.'

A few minutes later, Henry came back into the room. He was pushing a cart that was covered with a dust sheet. He parked it out of the way, then left again. A moment later he returned, pushing a rack with two spin-wheels. The spin-wheels were about the diameter of a car tire and they were mounted side by side. He parked it in front of Duncan and Christie. She noticed each of the wheels had pie-shaped sections and a pointer - similar to the prop wheel from the television show *Wheel of Fortune*. The wheel on the right was divided into eight sections. Duncan's name was written in every other section with her name in between. The wheel on the left was labeled *Sexual Act*, and it had numerous pie-shaped sections with different words and phrases. She read a few of them to herself. *Wheelbarrow, Golden Shower, Titty Fuck, Pocket Pussy, Missionary, Eating Balls, Anal, Prison Fellatio, Pile Driver, Doggie Style, Cowgirl, Eating Pussy, 69, Ankles Up, Head and Coprophagia.* She glared at Henry. 'What the hell is this perverted shit?'

Henry was setting up the camcorder. 'I'm not a director, so I came up with an idea to make the action flow. You two fuckers will take turns spinning the wheels, then act out what they fall on.'

'I know you don't think we're going to go along with this sick shit?'

'What the fuck are you crying about? Don't you like sex?'

'That has nothing to do with this. You're holding us against our will.'

'You have a chance to score big time, so stop acting like a faggot.' Henry walked over to the wheels and pointed at *Anal*. 'Check this shit out. If you land on here, you get to fuck Christie in the ass. And I doubt she was about to offer that before I came along.'

He charged towards Henry, but his cables jerked him back. 'You're going to pay for this, you sick fuck!'

'I knew you were a fucking faggot.'

'Fuck you, you crazy motherfucker! I will fucking kill you!'

Christie pulled Duncan back, then whispered in his ear. 'Remember our plan? We have to play along to get him to drop his guard.'

Duncan nodded. 'You're right. So what do you want to do?'

She started kissing him.

Henry turned off the camcorder, then sat in a chair. He lit a cigarette, then leaned back and watched the couple make out.

Christie got on her knees in front of Duncan and started massaging his penis. She looked at Henry. 'You can come join us if you like.'

Henry looked at her blankly and then smiled. 'Not my thing.'

'I thought this is what you wanted?'

'I just want to make a movie. A real filthy one for my personal collection.'

She was willing to fuck Duncan in front of Henry if that's what it took to get him to let his guard down, or let them go. She smiled. 'Then do it.'

'Do something nasty and I'll turn the camera on.'

She started sucking Duncan's flaccid penis.

Henry shrugged, clearly not impressed. 'This is boring.'

She knew she had to become more aggressive if Henry was going to fall for their act, so she lay on her back, then motioned to Duncan. 'Fuck me.'

Duncan felt humiliated as he crawled between her legs. He knew what they were doing was just an act, but it still made his stomach turn. He should be excited, he thought. Wasn't it every man's fantasy to fuck like a porn star? His penis wasn't getting hard, so she started stroking it with her hand as she talked dirty to him. She was being a good actress, he thought. *Was she actually getting into this?* His penis began to swell. He reached down to rub her clit and found that her pussy was wet. He now knew she was into it. Within seconds, his dick was hard as a rock. He didn't hesitate to shove it inside her. To his surprise, she wrapped her legs around his waist and began moaning with pleasure. He was no longer thinking about Henry as he thrust himself deep inside her. She was carrying on so much that he couldn't hold his load much longer. Seconds later, he pulled his dick out and squirted cum all over her stomach. His heart was racing and he was breathing heavily as he sat back on his knees.

Christie noticed Henry wasn't even watching—he was reading a book. She was relieved, thinking he really wasn't interested in them and hopefully would let them go. She sat up and looked at Duncan. 'He's not even paying attention.'

Duncan glared at Henry. 'I did what you wanted, so let us go.'

Henry looked up. 'No you didn't. There was nothing nasty about that.'
'What?'

'I said, there was nothing nasty about that.'

'Then what the fuck do you want?'

He turned on the camcorder, then walked over to the platform. 'I want *my* filthy movie. And since you don't have a clue to how to make it, we're going to do it my way.' He pointed to the wheels. 'All you have to do is spin these, then act it out. It's that simple.'

Duncan stood up. He felt bad about what happened and needed to prove that he wasn't a creep. 'Fuck you! We're not doing shit!'

'Oh really? Did you want to make a bet on that?' He looked at Christie. 'Ladies first.'

She shook her head. 'I don't want to.'

Henry walked to the cart that he had pushed in earlier and wheeled it over to the platform. He removed the sheet, revealing a disturbing sight. The top of the cart was covered in knives, scalpels, syringes, vials, hand tools, torches and medical supplies. The bottom shelf had a large cooler. 'We can do this the easy way, or hard way. I'll be honest, the day I've had, I'm kind of hoping for the latter but, I'll be nice, you can decide.'

'Why are you doing this? We don't even know who you are.'

Christie's heart skipped a beat when she saw what was on the cart. Up to this point, Henry was just a pervert with a few loose marbles, and now after seeing all the items on the cart and the trouble he had gone through to put everything together, *he's a fucking psychopath*. She still had hope though, thinking if she played along, she and Duncan could still take Henry out. 'Okay! I'll do it.'

'Smart girl.' He continued, 'I mean, yeah I'm disappointed we didn't get to do it the hard way but... Doesn't make you any less of a smart girl. So well done you. I could almost give you a pat on the head.'

She glared at him, desperate to tell him to *fuck off*, but said nothing. She spun the wheel labeled *Sexual Act*. She and Duncan watched in suspense as the pointer made a clicking sound. When it stopped, it landed on *Eating Balls*.

She glared at Henry with disgust. 'So I take it I have to suck his balls?'

'We won't know that until you spin the wheel on the right. Whoever's name that it stops on is the person who's receiving the sexual act, then you have to spin it again to see who's going to be performing it.'

'This is fucking stupid!'

'Just spin the damned wheel.'

She spun it. When it stopped, it landed on Duncan's name. 'Looks like Duncan will be getting his balls eaten. Now we just need to see who's going to do it.'

She looked at Henry like he was an idiot. It was bad enough she was being held against her will and being forced to perform sexual acts, but she didn't understand his obsession with the wheels. 'You know it's going to be me, so let me get it over with.'

'Hold up. I know you can't wait to taste some balls, but you might not even be the one doing it.' He gestured towards the wheel. 'Spin.'

'This is dumb.' She gave it a half-assed spin. It stopped on Duncan's name.

Henry looked at Christie. 'See, I told you that you might not be doing it. Now...' He turned to Duncan, 'Duncan has to eat his own balls.'

Duncan looked confused. 'What the fuck are you talking about? How can I eat my own balls?'

Henry looked at his watch. 'You have five minutes to do it.'

Duncan was getting frustrated. 'Do what? I don't understand?'

'Tick tock...'

'How am I supposed to eat my own balls?'

'Four minutes.'

'I can't reach them!' He bent forward to show he couldn't reach his groin with his mouth. 'Look! I don't have the dexterity! How in the fuck am I supposed to do it?'

'There is a man who's tried that move before.' He turned to Duncan, 'You know - apparently - if you try every day... Eventually you can stretch all the way down. So I've heard...' He laughed. 'Three minutes.'

'It doesn't matter how much time you give me. I can't do it, you fucking idiot!'

Christie pushed Duncan to the side. 'Don't get so upset. We have to make him feel comfortable if we're going to take his ass out.'

'I thought you weren't talking to me anymore?'

'We have to work together if we're going to get out of this.'

'You okay with having more sex in front of this guy? Because that's what he has planned for us.'

'What choice do I have?'

Henry yelled out. 'One minute left until I have to administer some motivation.'

Duncan glared at him. 'Motivation? What the hell does that mean?'

'It means you're ruining my movie. You know, I was watching your vanilla sex from down in my office. It was boring. I'm surprised you even managed to get a fucking erection and I'll wager she was bone dry with your half-assed attempts of *fucking*. Be grateful, I'm teaching you how to make a good porno that people will want to watch. So I suggest you stop conspiring with your little partner and get to eating some balls.'

'It's not going to happen, so I guess you're out of luck.'

Henry looked at his watch. 'Time's up.' He pulled out a remote with numerous buttons. When he pressed one, the cables started retracting into the holes in the platform. Duncan and Christie were panicking as they fought against them, but the cables were too strong, pulling them down to their backs.

'You don't have to do this! I'll cooperate!'

Henry had the power and both Christie and Duncan knew it. But - even so - before the games could continue, he would need to teach them a lesson on discipline and how they shouldn't argue with him when he told them to do something. He held up a scalpel. 'Where would you like to be cut?'

'Please don't do this.'

This was a good session. This is what his time with Agata should have been like, as opposed to the rushed mess that it actually was and what made it even better was...

The night is still young.

Matt Shaw

Part One

HOTEL MANAGEMENT

...Earlier

Chapter One

I like the simplicity behind Norman Bates' motel. I am envious of how easy it appears for him to both run the establishment and indulge in his murderous hobby. A one-man band running the whole place single handedly. It is simple, it is clean and - as such - it is painfully obvious that it is a work of fiction and that Robert Bloch didn't have a clue about running such a business. But then, maybe I am wrong? I run a hotel, the character of Bates ran a quiet motel. A business which - according to the character - used to be busy until a new highway was put in, taking the bulk of the traffic away from Bates' Motel. Maybe, before the highway was built, the motel was busy and Norman did have staff on hand to help him? A couple of people to man the desk, on a rota-ed basis, and a couple of cleaners to ensure the standard of the rooms didn't slip? I don't know. Maybe I should just enjoy it as a film and stop worrying about the little details? That's all it is after all, a film. Well, that's the version I like anyway. The film was entertaining, Bloch's book - not so much. I found the words clunky and descriptions lacking.

There was a knock on my office door which pulled me from my rambling thoughts. I leaned forward to my messy desk and reached for the television controller. Lifting it from the scattered papers, I pointed it to the screen - mounted on the adjacent wall - and hit the red button killing the picture in an instant. I can always catch up with the film later. It's not as though I haven't seen it before.

I set the controller back down upon the various bits of paperwork and turned to the (closed) office door.

'Come.'

The door opened and Agata leaned in. She is one of the many Polish workers I have working here. A pretty thing with blonde hair and blue eyes. A slim frame with breasts that wouldn't quite fill a handful.

'Your interview is here,' she said in an accent that I used to find endearing. Now I just find it irritating. A reminder that this country isn't what it used to be. Too many foreigners coming in, working here in order to earn a decent wage. A wage that they - usually - send home to loved ones. Mind you - on the other hand - thank God for the foreigners. At least they work. Unemployment stats have shot up again and all you see on the television is documentaries following a group of no-hopers as they live on benefits. It's embarrassing for two reasons. The first reason is that most of them are actually from this country. The second reason is they're being filmed doing all they can to actively avoid working yet continue claiming their fortnightly cash. A drain on society. I almost wish their benefits would stretch to a night in this hotel. Just one night. Breakfast not included.

'Send her in.'

11.am appointment.
Name: Pela.
Age: Thirty-two years old.
Gender: Female.

She had applied for the vacancy online and had sounded perfect for the role. A role that continually needed filling due to the high turnover of staff. The moment I read her details, I phoned her and invited her down for an immediate interview but - sadly - she wasn't able to do it due to prior commitments. That irritated me initially. I mean - she wanted a job, I offered her an interview. She should fit in with me, not the other way round. But then I realised I was being unreasonable. Struggling with bad network signal, we agreed to meet the following day (today) at 11.am. She is my only interview of the day and that is how confident I am that I will employ her.

A second knock at the door.

'Come in.'

The door creaked open and a *plain Jane* walked in. Not quite the beauty I had come to expect from the foreigners. I stood up and extended my hand.

A smile on my face reserved for those I wish to manipulate into thinking I am a nice man.

'You must be Peta,' I said as we shook. Her hand gripped mine limply. A girl lacking confidence. 'My name is Henry,' I told her. I gestured to the chair opposite from the one I had been sitting on.

'Pleased to meet you.' She took the seat as alarm bells began to ring in my head. Her accent was as lacking as her confidence. In fact, she sounds like all the other women born around these parts.

'That's a pretty name,' I told her as I fussed with a file of employment, opening it up to reveal the list of questions we had to go through.

'Thank you,' she said simply. I was hoping for a little more detail. For example, maybe where it originated from. Some kind of story behind it. 'Don't hear it too often.'

'It's Polish,' she said.

Bingo.

'Polish? You don't seem to have an accent?'

'My mum and dad are Polish. I was born in this country.'

I closed the file, hiding the questions that should have been posed. This is not the girl I am looking for. I have no work for her. Despite this revelation, I will still have to go through the motions but I can do it with a general, less structured conversation. Easier than going through the questions and making notes. I can't openly tell her that I'm not interested in giving her the job here because she is from this country. Not when there was a chance she could take me through the courts. Fucking Equal Opportunities.

'Did you move here when you were younger?' I asked.

'My mum and dad brought me over when I was about eight.'

'They're here too?'

'They are. They live in town. Dad runs a warehouse.'

I pretended to be interested. 'I'm surprised you're not working with him. I ended up in this business because of my parents. My father owned a hotel.'

'Carrying on his work.'

I smiled. 'Something like that.'

She is a definite no go, even if I had been tempted for a split second. Not only is she from this country originally - meaning friends who would notice her absence, what with always working - but she also has family here.

Friends might forget each other over time, if they don't keep in touch. Family never forgets. Even so - I need to keep up the pretence this is a job interview.

'So what attracted you to the hotel industry?'

Chapter Two

The pretend interview had lasted approximately thirty minutes. Agata, working the reception desk, knew the girl wouldn't get the job. She'd seen three interviews this week and all of the others had lasted at least an hour. One of the girls, from Bulgaria of all places, went even longer than that falling at only the last hurdle. She too had family living in this country.

I held the lobby door open for Pela. The cold air from outside rushed in causing her to wrap up in her coat and a shiver to run down my spine.

'Thank you for coming,' I told her. It was the polite thing to do even though I wasn't thankful for her attending. She had wasted my time. Or I had wasted my own time by not reading her application through properly. A mistake I won't be repeating when anyone else applies.

'Not a problem.'

'We'll let you know,' I told her. I won't be letting her know. I'll ignore it and hope that she gets the message through my silence.

'Do you have any idea when that will be?' she asked. There was a keenness in her voice - one which had been present for the duration of the interview which did, on some levels, impress me given the lack of confidence she appeared to have when she first walked in. But then, maybe I am misreading it? Maybe it is *desperation?*

'Probably within a week or so. I have a few more people to interview.'

'Okay.' She smiled, I think, for the first time. 'Well, thank you for your time.' And, with that - and another fake smile from me, she stepped out into the cold. I let go of the door, letting it slowly close of its own accord, and turned back towards my office - just off to the right of the reception

31

area.

Agata walked towards the end of the reception desk and called out to me, 'How was that one?' she asked.

'So so.' It wasn't any of her business and I was surprised she even asked. She usually kept to herself and only spoke to me when I asked her a question directly. I think - on some levels - she actually feared me. She was also overworked and most likely tired.

She hesitated before stuttering, 'W-Well…'

I turned to her, frustrated, and asked, 'What is it?'

I just wanted to go back to my office. The interview had annoyed me. I felt positive I had enough member of staff employed but - no - I was still without. It was still just Agata and myself. The last woman standing.

'I'm sorry and I know it is short notice but…'

'What do you want?' I snapped wishing she would just get to the point. If I was quick, I'd still be able to catch the end of *Psycho* on the television.

'I have an appointment next week that I really need…'

I cut her off. 'Cancel it.'

'Cancel it?'

'Yes.'

'But…'

'How much money did you send back to your folks last month? I don't need an exact figure but… Just rough. How much was it again?'

'About eight hundred.'

'And you know why you managed that?' She didn't answer. She knew what I was about to say. I had used the same line on her before when she had tried to get some time off. I don't get a day off. She doesn't get a day off. Not until we have some more staff anyway. 'You managed that because not only do you have a job but you also have somewhere to live rent-free. In exchange, all I ask is that you work the reception desk for me.'

The staff don't get to see the rest of the hotel. They only ever work the desk. I control the rest of the rooms. I always have and always will and the moment a staff member goes where they shouldn't… Well that is when I have to fire them.

The hotel has its secrets and they need to be kept.

Agata looked upset. Or was it annoyed? Frustrated maybe? I reassured her and said, 'Look - soon as we have a couple of more staff members so we can get a rota back in place… You can have days off. I promise. In the meantime, I'm paying you more for your time. It's not as though you're losing out. You get a free roof over your head and free food from the kitchen. You're getting a good deal but if you think you can do better somewhere else then by all means,' I gestured towards the hotel's entrance, 'you're more than welcome to leave.'

She didn't move.

I continued, 'I didn't ask people to leave. They were doing well with me and I liked having them around but... That's what happens when you employ people in a similar position to yourself. Occasionally they miss home too much and decide to go back. What could I do?'

A telephone on the reception desk started to ring, interrupting my speech. I glanced at it and nodded for Agata to answer it.

Lifting the handset to the phone she said, 'Reception. How can I help?' There was a pause as she listened to the needs of the room calling. Finally she put the handset back down. 'That was room ten. They wanted one of the club sandwiches taken up with a Coke.'

'Okay.' I turned back to the foyer and towards the kitchens. I stopped when I was midway across the floor. Without turning to Agata I told her, 'I'll see what I can do about your appointment, okay?'

'Thank you.'

'I'm not promising,' I finished as I left the foyer.

Chapter Three

I am the master of the club sandwich. Toasted bread with sliced poultry, fried bacon, lettuce, tomato and mayonnaise which is cut into quarters, or halves depending on my mood, that's held together by hors d'oeuvre sticks. On the side of the plate, I like to have some plain flavoured crisps. I prefer to avoid flavours, such as cheese and onion or salt and vinegar as I believe the sandwich has enough taste on its own. Add more flavours and you just taint the whole experience.

I took a step back and looked at the finished product and smiled smugly to myself. It's not a sandwich, it's a work of art. Almost a shame to eat it but knowing what it tastes like, it's a shame to *leave* it too. I moved the sandwich onto a large plate and put that onto a tray. I covered the food plate with a metal-lid to give the appearance of freshness. Also on the tray was the receipt - which needed signing to prove the guest made the order, and received it - and, lastly, was the drink they had requested; a can of Coke and a glass to pour it into.

I wouldn't normally have had to prepare the food for the guest. I'd have had a staff-member to deal with it but they too had left, having gone out back for a cigarette break and noticed one of the hotel's secrets... They had to go. Hotel manager, cleaner, caterer. What was the saying? Jack of all trades and master of none. I smiled to myself. Well, there's one I am master of...

I carried the food from the kitchen to the stairwell just beyond the kitchen door. The guest was in room ten which was on the first floor so there was no need to use the lift. It's not as though it's a hot meal in danger of going cold and the exercise will do me good. Carefully, I made my way up the stairs whistling as I did so. I might not have prepared the food before, when I had staff, but it was always me who delivered it. Again, I'm the one who goes down the corridors to the rooms - the staff were the ones who worked in the allotted areas behind the scenes. Those were the rules. Rules which - sadly - most couldn't get in their stupid heads. I don't know, maybe it was a language thing.

Top of the stairs and only a few doors away from the guest. I headed down the corridor. Next to each door - both sides of the corridor - was a small, locked cupboard about waist height. They looked out of place but they weren't for the guests' benefit. They were for *my* benefit. Inside each one were cleaning products, bin bags and fresh linen. At room number ten, I leaned down and carefully placed the tray down on the top of the cupboard. Another use for it - and one I hadn't considered when I actually put them there. Surprising really considering the idea of the cupboards was one born out of laziness. Easier to have cleaning products close to hand than having to wheel a trolley around stacked with all of the supplies.

I could hear the television through the door. The volume is so high I'm almost grateful the other rooms on this floor are pretty much empty. Otherwise I'd be having to deal with complaints as well as my usual tasks. Not that people tend to complain for very long here.

I raised a hand to the door and went to knock. I hesitated with my knuckles practically touching the wood as I came to realise what I was hearing through the door. That's not a family friendly film that's playing... Leaving the tray of food on the top of the cupboard I walked a little further down the corridor to the next door. I fished in my pocket for a set of keys and fumbled with them until I had the golden key in hand. The skeleton key which unlocks every room in the building. Without a second thought, I put the key in the lock and twisted. The lock clicked open allowing me the opportunity to open the door - which I did.

The other side of the door was not a room similar to the one which the guest next door was relaxing in. It was another corridor with a wall at the end of it. With the exception of some light spilling in through a series of spy holes on either side of the walls - peering into the rooms on the other side of the walls - the corridor was near pitch black. Knowing there was nothing on the floor to trip over, I stepped in and closed the door behind me. I walked to the first spy hole and peered through. There - on the other side of the wall - I could see the guest's room. He was lying on the bed with his trousers around his ankles. His eyes looked like they were fixed directly on me but I knew he didn't see me. More to the point I knew he was looking at the television which had been hung slightly to the side of this tiny hole. I felt a shimmer of disgust wash through me when I noticed he was frantically masturbating - clearly enjoying whatever film he had opted to watch. *Dirty fucker.* I'm used to cleaning up all kinds of disgusting stains when sorting the rooms and it is never pleasant but the *one* mark which never fails to offend me is the semen-stain. I find it disrespectful that these fucks come to my building and feel perfectly comfortable to shoot their loads over my bedsheets, floors, curtains… Whatever. Do they do this in their own home? I doubt it. Well - I don't doubt they masturbate but I bet any money in the world that they clean up after themselves. Here, they seem happy to shoot their load wherever they see fit and then just leave it to dry by itself. *Oh, never mind cleaning up, they have maids to do that.*

I guess he thought it was going to be a quick one or that the sandwich would have taken longer to prepare. Well, fuck him, if I am quick - I can knock on the door and ruin his fun before he ejaculates. Ruin the vinegar stroke for him. In a hurry to stop him from leaving me another mess to clear up, I left the narrow corridor and closed the door behind me - locking it once more - before heading back to the guest's room. I knocked on the door - hard.

Knock! Knock! Knock!

Chapter Four

I walked downstairs with the tray in my hands. Right up until the moment I walked onto the lobby floor, I had a huge grin on my face from what had just happened. The moment my feet touched the lobby floor though, the grin changed to a scowl - one which didn't go unnoticed by Agata who also noticed I still had the tray of food in my hands.

'Did he not like it?' she asked with genuine concern in her voice.

'Like it? He didn't order it.'

'What? He phoned down and…'

I set the tray down on the reception area so that I could berate my useless member of staff.

'You got the wrong room. He didn't order it. So now someone in this hotel is patiently waiting for a meal that isn't going to come. All we can do now is wait for said guest member to phone down with their complaint…'

'I'm sorry, I thought he said…'

'You need to listen more carefully. You need to repeat the room to the guest member to ensure it's the right one…'

'I could have sworn…'

'Just stop talking. You know how I hate to waste food and - more than that - you know how *fucking busy* I am. Like I don't have enough shit to do I have to go out and make up phantom orders.' I paused. She looked as though she were fit to burst into tears. 'The good news is,' I continued, 'I'm hungry so at least the sandwich hasn't gone to waste.' I told her, 'I'm going to my office. I don't expect to be disturbed. Okay?' Agata didn't say anything. She looked down to the floor - embarrassed. 'Okay?' I pushed for

37

an answer.

'Yes,' she said sheepishly.

I grabbed the tray from where I had put it and stormed through to my office. Once inside, I kicked the door shut and took a seat at my desk. The scowl disappeared from my face and the grin came back. Of course she had taken the order correctly but had I not made the scene, she would never have left me alone. She would have hassled me about the job interviews, desperate for me to take someone else on to take some of the pressure from herself. I have work to do and don't need her buzzing around. Now she thinks she has done something wrong, she'll stay out of my way and I can get my head down and get things accomplished. But first...

I lifted the metal lid from the plate and set it to one side. Hidden beneath was the guest's once-hard penis. I picked it up and it flopped to the side - no constant pump of blood to keep it erect. Shrunk too. The guy was a grower, not a show-er. With cock in hand I got up from the chair and walked to a small fridge in the corner of the room. I opened it up. On the top shelf was a selection of beverages - soft drinks and alcohol - and, beneath those... A selection of pieces cut from previous guests - mostly rotting away now. Keep -sakes that, despite their rotten state - I can't bring myself to dispose of. I set the penis down in its little glass jar and walked back to my seat. I sat down and reached for the remote control to the television. A quick press of the button the television flickered to life. *Psycho* was still on. Janet Leigh is about to bite it. My favourite scene and one often dissected (no pun intended) by movie-lovers all claiming to know something other people don't.

One of the biggest misconceptions is that you never see the knife blade penetrate Janet but that's rubbish. I watched the scene frame by frame and there is a shot where you do see the knife pierce the victim's stomach. It's not the only lie that has been spread about the film. I mean, some people still believe Alfred Hitchcock didn't direct this particular sequence. They firmly believe it was directed by the guy behind many of Hitchcock's title sequences, Saul Bass, but that's bullshit as is the lie Hitchcock didn't tell Janet Leigh her character was going to die meaning the whole sequence was a complete surprise to her. Another lie? To get realistic screams from Janet, Hitchcock used ice-cold water. One scene, so many rumours.

On screen the blood was running down the plug-hole. One truth about this scene is the rumour that it is not fake blood but actually chocolate syrup instead because it shows up better in the black and white format of film. When I first heard this, I laughed. Knowing the truth certainly takes the viciousness from the scene especially when you know the truth about the sound effects being used. It's not a knife being plunged into a person. It's a knife being plunged into a melon... I wonder if Hitchcock stabbed the melon himself? I reckon 'yes'.

With one eye on the screen still, I turned my computer on. A quick check of my emails and any new job applicants before I venture back to room ten and the clean-up that awaits. As the computer loads up and the emails come through, there are a number of spam messages mixed with a few new applicants from the job website. A quick flick through the latter and most of them are born and bred in this country. No good. Needs to be foreigners as I keep saying. Needs to be desperate people willing to do as I say and keep to the areas they're permitted in only. Needs to be people who I can make vanish easily if they step out of line or discover one of the many secrets of this hotel. The hotel's secrets need to be kept. I'll message these people telling them that the job is gone.

The new emails stop filtering through. No new potential applicants. A disappointing result, especially as I paid good money for the ad. Well - sorry Agata - no new staff members for you just yet... Another problem with the lack of applicants is it means she will be here a little longer too. Every day she is here, she becomes bolder in the way she talks to me and how she acts. I'm sure it won't be long before I need to let her go.

I leaned back in the chair and sighed heavily.

That hotel guest's face though... The shock... Almost takes away the disappointment from the lack of job applicants. Almost.

Part Two

THE HOTEL
AND ITS STAFF

Matt Shaw

Chapter One

I entered room 10 for the second time that evening. This time I was not met with the fake moans and groans of some whore on the screen, getting rammed hard by a steroid-taking junkie. Nor was I met with the sight of a middle-aged man having a quick one off the wrist. Instead I was met with his unblinking gaze and pained expression, frozen onto his pale face. He was lying on the bed. The sheets beneath him were bathed in red, both from where his penis had been severed and from the wound in his neck. The knife used still sticking from the latter.

I put the cleaning materials down on the floor next to the bed. I say cleaning materials but - yeah - mainly it is black sacks for the stained bedding sheets. There is also a plastic sheet, tainted in dried blood from previous guests who'd ended up being wrapped in it. I set the plastic down on the floor, next to the bed, and then grabbed the hotel guest by his ankles. With a little effort, I pulled him from the bed. He landed - hard - on the plastic sheeting with a heavy thud. I'm not worried about complaints from the room below seeing as most of that floor is empty. With him out of the way, I can start by stripping the bed down and putting the sheets in the bag. They won't be cleaned, they will be incinerated in the furnace down in the cellar along with the body. The cost of the room easily covers replacement sheets and - sometimes - the guests have a wallet full of cash that I use too, along with credit cards which are used to book other hotel rooms and flights. Make it look as though they've not only left my premises but gone on to book elsewhere too.

They were here, officer, but they checked out early this morning.

The blood seeped through to the duvet but not through to the mattress. On the occasions when it did leak through to the actual bed, I just made sure the replacement sheets were of dark colours to ensure the stains remained hidden. To this day I haven't had anyone removing the sheets to check out the bare bones of the bed. First time for everything though but - when it does happen - I'll just apologise. And then I'll kill them.

I scrunched the bedding up and put it into one of the black sacks. Tomrorow, I'll put the fresh bedding on as it will be dry by then. At least it would be dry enough to not let the dampness seep through. More than that, it would look inviting to the tired traveler. They'd never have suspected anything had happened there, let alone someone being murdered. I nodded to myself; a job well done.

I glanced down to the body. Thankfully he is (was?) an average sized person. Not too hard to move. I wrapped the plastic sheeting around him and stood back up, satisfied that everything was going to plan. But then - why wouldn't it? This isn't my first time.

I walked over to the wall where the television hung. Just behind it, tucked out of sight, was a little button. A simple press and the wall slid across revealing the narrow corridor I had stood in earlier as I spied on the occupant. With the secret door open, all I needed to do was lump the body from Point A through to Point B. Another button press, once the body was in the corridor and - even easier - gravity would take care of the rest for me.

I went back over to where the body lay on the plastic sheeting and pulled the two sides together. With a little bit of folding, it wasn't long before the guest looked like nothing more than an overly large parcel - albeit with feet poking from one end but that was a necessity; I needed something to pull him by.

I looked across through to the narrow corridor on the other side of the wall where I needed to drag him. That short distance suddenly appeared a lot further. Should have killed him closer to the wall. Less of a distance to drag the fucker.

I sighed.

No sense bitching about it. It is what it is and I can't exactly leave him here or get someone to help me. I stood up straight and did a couple of stretches. Back in the days when I used to gym, stretches were important before any strenuous activity. They save you from pulling muscles, or worse - ripping them.

Stand up straight. Left hand to left ankle. Pull ankle up until back of the heel is touching your rear. Stretch. Release. Right hand to right ankle. Repeat. Good. Left arm up in the air to the side of your head. Grab bicep with right hand, your right arm resting on the top of your head. Lean body to the right. Get a click from one or more of your joints. Release. Same again but right arm up and left hand on bicep. Lean body to the left. Another bout of clicks. Relax. Shake out your arms and legs. And - you're ready.

Scrunching the two corners of the plastic sheeting up into both of my hands, I grabbed the body by its ankles and pulled backwards, dragging him towards the hidden chamber. The weight pushing down on the plastic sheet actually helps; the plastic making him slide easier. By the time we are in the next room, I realise I was moaning for little reason. Despite his weight, he was actually a piece of cake to move. But then, thinking back, I always find this to be the case - certainly since dragging them when they're on the plastic. Before I used any wraps, I usually found that their clothes scrunched up and caused more resistance to pull against. Definitely easier with plastic.

In the next room I released him when I had his body where it needed to be. Ensuring no bits of plastic were left overhanging into the bedroom, and I was standing away from the trap door, I pressed another button on the wall. Within an instant the wall slid back across, hiding this room from view once more, and a trap door beneath the body swung open. The body dropped from sight. I heard it bang against the sides of the shaft as it dropped through to the cellar. A second later, the trap doors swung shut again.

'Shit...' An overhead light was supposed to come on when the trap door closed so I wasn't left in complete darkness but - not for the first time - it failed to illuminate. *Fucking brilliant.* Could be that the bulb has fried. Or it could be that the guy who helped build this had fucked up. Times like this I wished I had kept him around so that I could have asked him to fix it but - yeah - no sense crying over spilt milk.

Feeling along the walls, I stumbled my way through to the door. I'll pop back to Room 10 and deal with the rest of the clean-up in there and then - when I'm finished, I'll head on down to the cellar. The whole process should take me a little under an hour.

Give or take...

Chapter Two

The cellar was open plan as per my designs. Along the length of the wall was a work-station similar to one to be found in a busy garage. An array of tools hung from the wall, within easy reach. The wooden worktops, stained with dark red. On the far wall - jutting out from the centre - was the furnace. Always lit, with flames roaring within flicking violently from side to side, giving off an intense heat.

From the top floor right down to the cellar, a line of trap-doors had been built into the floors. One button press caused all of them to open allowing anything and everything to fall freely from the top floor right down to where I was standing now with minimum fuss, just the occasional bang as whatever was falling hit the edges of the trap as it passed through.

'Hello, yes, this is room number thirteen,' I remember one guest calling down to the reception. 'I would like to report a banging noise from the room next door.'

Agata had reported the complaint to me. I told her that it was the pipes and to just apologise to the guest. Truth of the matter had been, two boisterous guests had been offed on the top floor. On the way down, through the trap doors, they must have hit the sides as was often the case. On this occasion, and indeed when other people had complained at other times, I had told Agata to offer him a free breakfast for the following morning as way of an apology even though I knew he - like the two guests from the top floor - wouldn't see the morning in order to collect.

All complaints will be heard.

All complainers will be shown to the cellar.

The cellar floor, below the last of the trap doors, was heavily dented although made from concrete. Many bodies had dropped from top to bottom and some had been heavier than others. The heavy ones sure did leave their mark over time, not that it really mattered.

With the exception of the work-station and the furnace, there was nothing else in the cellar. For a while I had considered getting a table of some description. I thought it would be easier to work on the body, cutting them into smaller and more manageable pieces, if they were up higher - as opposed to having me crouch to the floor to cut at them. But I figured that, by the time I got them up on the table in the first place... I could have potentially cut through most of the limbs anyway. Especially when dealing with the fat cunts who'd dropped down here.

When dealing with the bodies, I grabbed the tools from the workstation and dropped to my knees next to where the bodies had landed with their bones all broken and bent out of shape due to the impact. Sometimes they land on their heads. The heads either explode like rotten melons or the necks snap yanking the head to a ninety-degree angle. It's funny - some of the shapes you see the fuckers land in.

Once on my knees next to where they lay, I'd set about cutting them into smaller chunks. These pieces would then be tossed into the roaring furnace.

Sometimes I find myself standing at the open doorway of the furnace and just staring into the flames. I imagine them to be the flames of an Eternal Hell, licking away the flesh of the sinners. Skin changes colour. Skin blisters. Skin bubbles and pops... The aroma reminiscent of a barbecue on a hot summer's day as meat sizzles away - not that it had always been like that. When I had first started doing this, I didn't think to shave off the hair first. Hair burning is a smell that lingers, insulting the nostrils, for days. Sometimes longer. Now I shave the hair and use it to stuff up pillows that seem to have lost their plumpness over the years.

I don't burn the clothes either. At least, not all of them. Clothes that aren't ripped or torn by the violent end met by the wearer are salvaged. In this instance, all bodies are stripped of what they are wearing. The clothes are washed thoroughly and then stuffed into black bags. These bags are not for the garbage men to collect though. These bags are for the charity shops. No sense wasting them when they could go to someone less fortunate.

The clothes which have been damaged in the struggles though, yeah, they're burned in the flames.

The flames. Occasionally I see beyond them and I see the remnants of bone but - it's not often. The way the flames dance for me - it's hypnotic and hard to see anything else. One minute I'm standing there, admiring the beautiful dance and the next, I'm wondering if the same fate awaits me. Are Hell's flames waiting to lick the flesh from my own body?

Chapter Three

I tossed the last piece of the victim into the furnace and breathed in deeply. The sweet smell of burning flesh which - for some reason - tends to disgust many people going by literary works and movies. I don't know why. I like the smell. As the skin cracks and blisters, the aroma reminds me of beef. As the flames start licking away at the fat, I'm reminded of pork under a grill. Occasionally, the sweet smell has made my stomach rumble and a craving for meat to pang from within my belly. Before now, in similar situations to where I find myself now, I've gone upstairs only to be confronted by a hotel guest, or staff member, wanting to know what was cooking.

'It smells amazing,' they'd say.

'Cooked it myself,' I'd reply with a wink. But I would never let them know what it was, be it for real or a made up menu, in case they asked for a portion themselves.

With a metal pole taken from where it leaned against the wall, I pushed the furnace door shut. I set the pole back against the wall and walked over to the workstation where I grabbed a bucket of water which I filled at a small sink (cold water only) at the far end of the workstation. As the water splashed into the empty container, I added some soap and watched as it tried to froth despite the lack of heat. A quick clean up of the gore beneath the trap door and I would be done. Forty-five minutes. Either I'm getting quicker or it had been a smart move on my part when I recently ordered in new blades and cutting tools. The others had been getting somewhat blunt as the months went by and the bodies increased. Never easy for cutting.

I turned the tap off as the water level reached the lip of the bucket.

Carefully, I took a hold of the handle and carried it over to the puddle of ripped flesh, blood and bone fragment. There is no precise art to this...

I tipped the water from bucket to floor, splashing away the mess in a greasy, red river. This part of the cellar, thanks to a little tweaking, was on the slightest of slopes that led to a little drain I had built in specially for the occasion. One, maybe two, buckets of water was all that was needed to encourage the excess mess to run off down into the drain. The drain itself being filled with lime - something I replaced on a weekly basis by removing the grate and shovelling more down into the hole. The lime doesn't get rid of the dead bodies. The movies have it wrong. But - it does help with the stink of decomposing flesh so - I still use it.

Satisfied with how the floor looked, I set the bucket down. I need to get back upstairs to check on Agata. Make sure she is okay and find out if any more guests have checked in. Some of the rooms are still full but - unusual for this time of the year - most are still vacant. Still, not a problem. It gives me time to go from room to room to see if the guests are deserving of life or a trip to the cellar. The bigger the asshole, hiding out in the room, the more painful I make their death. The more innocent they look, the better the breakfast they get in the morning.

Shaking myself free from the protective clothing I wore over my clothes, to prevent me getting covered in gore, I headed for the cellar door and with each step I took towards the door, I whistled a happy little tune. Funny how a little mess, followed by a quick clean-up, can alleviate the day's stress. With any luck, the rest of the evening will be plain sailing.

*

The cellar opens up into the foyer. You could say that I'm practically hiding my hobbies in plain sight. I tell the staff working the reception desk that it's my private area and that I've got a gym and relaxation area down there. Just as they live in the hotel, so do I. On occasion I've had one or two people ask if they can see it. I always say no but - with the exception of Agata - they've all seen it now. Funny how that worked out.

I stepped into the foyer half-expecting to hear Agata calling out to me. Nothing of importance - just a hello, or words similar. Nothing. I glanced across to the desk and she wasn't where she was supposed to be stationed. I frowned to myself. Not like Agata to leave her station. Especially when she knew I was going to the cellar and it was only the two of us running the show. What if a guest had come in? Or what if someone phoned down to the reception area with a request. Not very good customer service. Unless - maybe she had to go to the bathroom? As far as I can see it, that's the only forgivable reason for her to have left her station.

I started towards my office at the opposite side of the foyer only to freeze mid-step. The door was open and - worse yet - I could see Agata sitting at my desk. Her eyes fixed on the computer screen.

What the fuck?

Resisting the urge to shout out - asking what the hell she was doing in my office - I stormed across the foyer and burst through the doorway. She spun towards me with a look of shock on her face. I noticed the screen was loaded up onto my emails.

'I'm sorry I...'

'Shut up.' I stepped up to the computer and leaned down to get a closer look as to what exactly she was reading. 'Ah.' She was going through the job applicants. Clearly she is desperate to know if I have anyone in mind yet. I sighed heavily. It must be hard for her, working with just me. She's been around for a while now - watching staff come and go. One of the hardest workers I've ever had and one of the best at sticking to the rules in place for working here. 'I'm sorry,' I told her. She frowned at me, confused by my words. 'I've been promising you more staff and yet - still nothing. You must be tired of working so hard for me...'

'It is tiring,' she said cautiously before quickly adding, 'but I like it here.'

'You know what... I've been hard on you. How about you have the rest of the evening off?'

'But who will work the reception desk?'

'I've nothing else to do. I'll sort it.'

Her face lit up. 'Really?'

I nodded. 'Really.'

'That would be...'

I stopped her in her tracks. 'And... Did you want to see down in the cellar?' I asked. 'The relaxation area down there will help you unwind. A bigger television than the one which is in your room. Extensive blu-ray library. Games. Gym equipment. Even got a little hot tub down there which you're more than welcome to use on the understanding you don't tell the new staff members when I do finally employ them.' I continued, 'Think of it as a thank you for working so hard for me. What do you say? Fancy it?'

She nodded. I couldn't help but smile. The fly lands in the sticky web. The spider waits for it to tire itself out and then pounces.

'Come on,' I told her. 'I'll show you down there and then - it's up to you what you do with your free time.'

I leaned across her and flicked the computer screen off, hiding the emails. She stood up.

'I'm sorry for...'

'Honestly, don't mention it.' I smiled at her. She smiled back.

'Thank you.'

Never smile at a crocodile...

'No, Agata. Thank *you.*'

It's a shame to say goodbye to Agata but she has crossed a line. It's a shame not just because she is the last of my staff members but because she was a damned fine worker but - I can't have people thinking it is okay to snoop around areas that are off-limits. What if she had opened the small fridge in there?

'Actually, before we go down to the cellar - can I just ask that you pop to the kitchens and grab me a quick drink?'

She nodded. 'Certainly. Anything in particular?'

I smiled. 'Something hot.' I paused a moment. 'I'm looking forward to seeing your face when you see the cellar,' I told her.

'I'm excited,' she said, still smiling.

'Me too,' I flashed her another grin as my mind stirred up old memories of previous staff members I had been forced to lay off. 'I can't wait to see your face when you see it down there,' I told her again.

Part Three

SACKED

Matt Shaw

Adam and Maja
by
Sam West

'You sure no one see us?' Maja asked.

'Yeah, I'm sure,' Adam replied.

'I not want lose job.'

Adam resisted the urge to roll his eyes; Maja was Polish and her English was crap. Adam was Slovakian and he considered his own English to be impeccable.

She's a thick, lazy cunt, he thought in English as if to prove the point of his own superiority.

Still, it wasn't exactly her mind he was after. Of all the chicks that worked here, she had to be the hottest. His dick was rock hard just thinking about what he was going to do to her in the honeymoon suite. He knew the room was off-limits, just as the other rooms were too, to the staff members but... Their own sleeping quarters were full of other staff, all of whom were sleeping. Besides, he was so pent up, it probably wouldn't take very long to get in there and get finished...

He slid the key into the lock, pulling her body against his at the same time. His mind reeled at the feel of her; she was fucking *gorgeous*. Well, the face wasn't all that – her nose was too big and her jaw too heavy – but who cared with those tits. They were like fucking m*elons*.

He had to lean down to kiss her as she was so short and his free hand curled around one of those luscious mounds. His fingers sunk into them – no plastic there – and one-handed he fumbled with the top-buttons of her white shirt. Suddenly, the door gave way beneath his shoulder and he lurched sideways into the empty void, almost falling over and taking Maja with him.

Still with his mouth clamped down on hers, he fumbled for the light-switch and walked her backwards towards the huge, heart-shaped bed in the centre of the room, pushing her down on top of it.

'Take off your clothes,' he ordered. No way was he doing it in the dark and missing out on the sight of those tits.

Her short, bleached blonde hair stuck up in tufts around her flushed face as her fingers obligingly hovered over the buttons of her shirt. He licked his lips, then almost howled in frustration when her fingers went slack.

'If someone catches us…'

Frustration mingled with horniness. Just get your fucking kit off already.

'I've told you, no one is gonna catch us, the room isn't booked 'til tomorrow. I stole the key and made a copy of it, the dumb cunt on reception didn't even notice it was gone.'

Maja didn't look convinced; the stupid bitch probably didn't even understand what he was saying. Doubt flickered across her heavy features and Adam's frustration gave way to anger. The fucking tart had been giving him the eye since she'd started at the hotel three weeks ago and now the time had come for to make good on her promise. He pushed her backwards on the bed, tearing at her shirt.

'Adam,' she gasped as he finally freed those tits.

Whether the gasping of his name was a signal for him to slow down, or whether it was from arousal, he didn't know or care. Her tits were every bit as good as he'd thought they'd be. Better. Her nipples were small and blood-red and greedily he sucked on one, mashing her tits together amidst the ruins of her bra.

So intent was he on the job at hand, that he almost screamed when a familiar voice spoke up;

'It is against hotel policy for staff to access guest areas.'

Maja *did* scream, a high-pitched squeal that momentarily distorted in his eardrums.

'What *the fuck*,' Adam said, rolling off Maja.

Henry's six-foot frame towered over them, his hands clasped behind his back and Adam blinked up at him in confusion. How the hell had *he* got in here? Adam was positive he had locked the door behind them; it was like the big boss-man had magicked himself in through the *fucking walls*.

'Take off your clothes, Maja.'

Surely he hadn't heard right? Surely Henry had meant to say, *put your clothes back on...*

Adam was dumbstruck. Henry was usually so mild-mannered, so polite. But now, looking up at him, it was like looking at a different man. Gone was his customary, bland, half-smile, and in its place was the kind of smile that Adam had only seen within the walls of the mental asylum in Slovakia where his senile Grandfather was housed.

'Are you deaf as well as stupid, you Polish cunt, I said take off your fucking clothes.'

Next to Adam, Maja began to cry, wrapping her opened shirt tightly around her chest. He got to his feet, finding his voice at last:

'I'm so sorry, this has all been a terrible mistake, I think we should go...'

'You're not going *anywhere*, Adam Hornik. Hornik by name, horny by nature. Tell me, does Maja know about your wife and kid back in Slovakia?'

By now, Adam was too frightened to be cross at his boss's admission. There was something deeply wrong with Henry; he had flipped his lid, there was no doubt about it.

'Look, Henry,' he said above Maja's wailing, 'We really are sorry, we didn't mean any harm...'

His words trailed off when Henry's hands came into view and he saw the axe he was holding. Casually, he rhythmically smacked the neck of it in the palm of his other hand. His blue eyes shone with mirth and Adam felt his stomach curdle.

'Well come on then, Adam Hornik and Maja Glinsky, you came here to fuck, so don't let me stop you. I have to say, you both have to be two of the sexiest pot-washers in the history of the world. Adam; so tall, dark and handsome, Maja, so pale, blonde and curvy. I can't wait for the show to start.'

This is a joke, just a horrible, sick joke.

Adam felt dampness on his cheeks and realised he was crying.

'Please,' he sobbed, 'you've made your point, please just *stop*.'

Henry raised the axe. 'Stop? But we haven't even started.'

The axe came swinging down and Adam only just managed to roll to one side in time. The damn thing narrowly missed his thigh by a matter of inches and he fell off the heart-shaped bed, landing with a *thump* on his backside. Numb terror seeped into his limbs, rendering them useless as he watched Henry.

He's a psycho a god damn motherfucking psycho!

Henry wiggled the axe to dislodge it from the bed. The metal head exited the mattress innards and surfaced from the white, silk sheets. Adam rediscovered the use of his limbs just as Henry raised the axe once more.

'Run, little piggy, run for your life, the big, bad wolf is coming to get you.'

Adam didn't have to be asked twice. He was up and running, not sparing a second thought for Maja who was still on the bed, screaming.

He threw himself against the door, a strange wailing sound reaching his ears. Dimly, he was aware that the sound was coming from him. His last thought before the searing pain struck was;

The key, where's the fucking key?

Pain exploded in his left leg and he let out an unholy wail, buckling to the floor. This can't be happening, he thought incredulously. Was this how his life was going to end? It didn't make any sense.

He clutched his damaged leg, horrified at the sight of the blood pumping out to the side of his knee. His stomach roiled and the room took on a grainy, black and white quality.

No, don't pass out…

Clutching the wound with one hand, he reached up above his head in search of the door-handle.

Fuck, too high.

Henry loomed over him; still smacking the bloodied neck of the axe in the palm of his hand. Adam's own blood from the axe-head sprayed him in the eyes, making him blink.

'The door's locked, you dumb cunt, you're not going anywhere.'

Adam began to blubber. 'Please don't kill me, I'll do anything you want, pleeease…'

His words gave way to tears.

'Anything? You'll do anything?'

It took a moment for the words to sink into Adam's brain. Could he really have been thrown a lifeline?

'Yes, yes, anything, just please, don't kill me.'

'Okay, then. If you didn't want me to kill you, all you had to do was ask.'

Adam forced himself to look into the monster's eyes. 'Can I go now?' he sobbed pathetically.

'Of course. But only if you help me to kill Maja, and if you promise not to tell.'

'I promise,' he gabbled, not daring to believe his luck.

'That's great, I knew you were different, Adam, I knew you'd understand. So, would you mind dealing with Maja? I want you to strip naked, and then I want you to help Maja out of her clothes.'

'But my leg,' he said unthinkingly, wincing at the mere thought of dragging his black work trousers over the bleeding gash in his leg.

'The wound isn't that deep. Come on, Adam, are we friends or not?'

'Yes, friends,' he said, unbuckling his belt.

'Good man.'

Adam undressed to the soundtrack of Maja's wailing. Henry was right, the wound wasn't as deep as he'd first thought. Blood still flowed from the gash, and it hurt like merry fuck, but it wasn't bone-deep.

Just do as he says, and I maybe I'll live.

Once he was naked, he made his way over to Maja on the bed. The stupid cow had pulled herself into the foetal position at the head of the bed, she hadn't even *tried* to escape.

Yeah, well, maybe not so stupid. It's not like it did me much good.

'Do not do, Adam, he lie,' she said in her customary shit English.

Her words angered him, and he yanked her arms away from her chest, exposing her breasts.

She's fucking right.

Refusing to give in to the doubt, and hiding behind a convenient wave of anger, he tore at her clothes, ripping her little black work-skirt off her body. He tugged the white cotton knickers down her legs, taking the sensible black work-shoes with them.

She looked up at him with big, tear-filled blue eyes and Adam pushed the guilt all the way down to the darkest corner of his soul.

'Nice. Very nice. Adam, lie on your back. Maja, suck his cock like you've never sucked cock before.'

Adam lay down and stared up at the ceiling, bracing himself for the sensation of a hot, wet mouth to wrap around his shaft.

Nothing happened.

'Fine, have it your way, Maja. I *was* going to play nice.' Henry loomed over him on the bed, blocking out the view of the ceiling. 'Adam, grab hold of Maja's legs and hold them open. I've got her shoulders.'

59

Maja put up a fresh fight, bucking and squirming when he grabbed her ankles and tugged. Together, he and Henry flipped the sobbing girl onto her back and Adam prised open her legs.

'No, Adam, he lie!' she screamed between sobs.

'I don't know about you, Adam, but this bitch is giving me a headache.'

Henry let go of the girl's shoulders and she sat bolt upright, screaming. He brought the axe swinging down into her face, the edge of the blade hitting her square in the mouth. She flopped back down again, silent at last, save for the wet, gurgling sounds. The axe had cut through the outer corners of her lips so that her mouth now stretched from ear to ear. Immediately, her newly carved mouth welled with blood and Henry grabbed her discarded knickers, shoving them into the gaping wound.

'Fuck her, Adam.'

Adam found he was shivering; a distant part of his mind warning him that he had gone into shock. He looked blankly down at the mutilated woman whose legs he still held, then back up at Henry.

'Sometime today,' he said conversationally, 'before I decide to use this axe on you.'

Adam came to himself slightly.

Do or die…

'Would you mind if I hid her face?' he asked in a voice that sounded remarkably calm to his own ears.

'Do what you want. Just get on with it.'

So Adam fisted the silk sheet by the side of her head and dragged the material over her face.

Better.

Henry no longer had to hold her down; that blow with the axe had really knocked the stuffing out of her. Ignoring Henry standing over them he concentrated hard on Maja's body, focusing on the slit of her neatly trimmed pussy and oversized tits that trembled with her hitching sobs. Her labia was bright red, like her nipples, and despite the wound in his knee and the abject horror of his situation, his cock was growing hard.

Instinctively, he reached down to stroke his thickening shaft, pushing the feeling of self-loathing down into that dark place he didn't know he had within him. Because if he could get hard right now, then what the fuck did that say about him?

No, don't think. Just do.

He reached out with his free hand to part her dry slit, inserting a finger inside of her.

So tight…

And then he was positioning his cock at her entrance, shoving himself inside. The shock of the hot, tight vagina wrapped around his cock reverberated through his entire body, making him shudder with sensory overload. She just felt so fucking *good*, and it wasn't long before he was ramming into her at speed, lost in the moment. The pain in his leg lessened and his balls tightened with each hard shove. Dimly, he was aware of Henry talking to him;

'You dirty fucking bastard, I can't believe you actually did it. I like your style, Adam, it's a shame I'm going to have to kill you.'

Adam stopped mid-thrust. Surely he'd misheard; they'd had a deal…

'No, please, don't…'

He squealed when Henry fisted his hair, yanking his head back and pulling him to his knees, his cock exiting Maja's vagina with an audible *pop*. Caught off-guard, he flailed his arms wildly to keep his balance.

The glint of the descending axe flashed across his fear-widened eyes, followed by searing pain. It enveloped him in a blaze of agony, knocking his breath out and sending him sprawling. He clutched the stump that had once been his cock, his hands instantly soaked through with his pumping blood.

My cock, he thought in disbelief.

His mouth twisted open in a silent scream, his howl of agony lodged in the pit of his guts.

Then the axe blows rained down. Again and again they came down; chopping, hacking, dismembering, slicing. The pain was unspeakable, holding him enthralled in its grip, leaving him beyond tears, beyond rational thought.

He died a few seconds after the axe severed his head from his neck in one clean chop. For the briefest of moments there was a sensation of soaring through the air, and he felt so *light*. A distant, still comprehending part of his mind loosely understood that Henry was holding his head aloft, affording him a final glimpse of his body…

Or what was left of it. The last thing he saw was his own bloody torso lying on the bed, floating amidst a sea of red. His flattened, mangled limbs were no longer attached, and pink coils of intestines had escaped the confines of his stomach, spilling out over shiny white bone and red clumps of meat.

The stench of shit hit his nostrils as his brain finally blinked out, and the last thing he heard was Henry laughing.

During the frenzied attack, Maja had managed to roll off the bed to avoid being dismembered along with Adam. She had hauled herself into a sitting position, one arm coiled tightly around her legs, the other clutching the silk sheet to her ruined face.

Dlaczego to się dzieje? she thought in her native tongue. *Why is this happening?*

The room had turned red. Adam's blood spurted up in great, red arcs – grotesque waterfalls that soaked everything in sight. Walls, ceiling, the tasteful, art-deco furniture; nothing was spared the glistening, dripping red.

And still the blood pumped and spurted and gushed and oozed.

Maja couldn't take it anymore. Her mind wobbled precariously over the cliff-edge of insanity as she shut her eyes and rocked on the floor, trying to block out the horror.

'Open your eyes Maja, I promise I won't hurt you,' Henry said, his voice filled with laughter.

She didn't open her eyes, but she became aware that Adam had stopped screaming and the deadly *thunk* of the axe hacking through flesh and bone had ceased.

'If you don't look at me, I'll rip off your eyelids.'

She opened her eyes. 'Please don't hurt me,' she begged, but the words came out all wrong as her ruined mouth no longer allowed her to speak.

'Peekaboo.'

Despite the agony of her torn open face and the fact she was close to drowning on her own blood that seeped down the back of her throat, she let out shrill scream. Henry was holding up Adam's handsome head by his black hair. His lifeless eyes stared down at her and his mouth was twisted wide open in a silent scream.

She turned away from the grisly sight, babbling incoherently, crawling away from the blood-drenched psychopath.

'You're not going *anywhere.*'

Pressure in the small of her back forced her down face-first onto the floorboards, flattening her out like a rug. Fiery agony exploded in her face, but she hardly cared. All she wanted to do was to get away from Henry, to never have to look into his glittering blue eyes again.

Hands roughly grabbed her shoulders, forcing her onto her back. Caught by surprise like that she found herself staring up into Henry's face...

And her mind lurched some more, threatening to unravel completely. Clamped between his teeth like a cigar in the red-sheened face dangled a dripping lump of meat; it took her a moment to realise it was Adam's cock.

Before she could draw breath to scream, Henry plucked the lump of flesh from his grinning mouth and pushed it into her ruined face.

'Suck his cock, bitch,' he laughed, grinding it against her clenched teeth through the flapping skin that once been her cheeks.

With his other hand, he prised open her jaw as if she were a dog that had to swallow a pill, and rammed the severed penis into her mouth. She squealed in terror – the thing tasted foul, so much worse than the metallic tang of her own coppery blood. It tasted of blood and sweat and shit and her stomach heaved. He wiggled it around in her mouth and she groaned in misery. After a minute or two, he seemed to grow bored and he flung the penis across the blood-soaked room.

She lay there sobbing with her eyes tightly shut, her face a fiery mess of agony.

'Open your eyes, Maja, don't make me hurt you.'

She might've laughed at that, in another life. Even though doing so went against every natural instinct she possessed, she opened her eyes. Maybe, if she was a good girl, he might spare her...

She found herself staring into Adam's deep brown eyes. For a brief second, she allowed herself the fantasy that it really *was* Adam, that he was alive and well. She clung onto that girlish infatuation that had gotten her through the countless, long, boring shifts in the hot, steamy kitchen. Because unbeknown to Adam, she had been madly in love with him; just one tiny smile from him used to make her heart sing, and his long, lingering looks used to leave her weak at the knees.

The face of the love of her life loomed closer, and she concentrated on his beautiful brown eyes, refusing to look any lower.

I love you, Adam, she thought as his cold, distorted lips pressed down on her mess of a mouth.

She felt the clammy flesh of his face drag downwards, wincing and shivering as Henry dragged the severed head over her quivering breasts. It went lower, trailing down her flat stomach and finally coming to rest at her groin. Her thighs were prised apart and she felt a firm pressure against her vagina.

The pressure intensified, making her squeal in alarm.

'Are you a virgin, Maja? You're very tight, Adam's head is *never* going to fit.'

She raised her trembling head in time to watch Adam retrieve his axe. He strode back over to her as Maja kicked the head away and tried to scramble away from him on her backside.

Mesmerised, she watched the axe come slicing down through the air and connect with her groin.

Pain exploded in her midriff and she flopped backwards, her entire body jerking like she had been electrocuted.

'Watch,' he said, yanking a silk-covered pillow off the bed and using it to prop up her head.

Maja's mind was not what it had once been, and strange, guttural noises escaped her destroyed mouth. She lay in an ever-growing pool of blood and she no longer fully understood what she was seeing or what was happening.

Her torso jerked and slipped around in the blood as he did something to her down below. She couldn't see much anymore – everything had dimmed and the pain had mercifully dialled down a notch as she drifted into unconsciousness.

'*Now* it fits,' Henry said.

Maja didn't understand the words, she was fading fast.

In the final moments before she died, she weakly stretched out a blood-soaked hand. She glimpsed Henry leaning over the television, and the entire back wall appeared to lurch sideways.

Then there was just blackness.

Trinkets

by

Ryan Harding

Pawel returned from the darkness thinking of the goddess and trinkets, same as he had before he had plunged into the nothingness. It was difficult to reconcile this with the tools which now hung overhead, far more blunt and serrated brands of trinkets. It was a room he had never seen, but in his confusion he could have almost believed he must have found a secret portal back to Poland in room 213.

Awareness seeped back into his head like carbon monoxide into a suicide's car.

Carbon monoxide?

That concept held him for some reason. There hadn't been carbon monoxide in 217, no, but he'd noticed something else. As soon as he became aware, it was like he'd somehow dematerialized and dropped through the floor, to eventually awaken in this chamber.

He was solid again now, the ground equally so beneath him and the wall behind him. There were no windows, just harsh light overhead that initially kept him from opening his eyes more than a slit. It suggested an operating room, which was further enhanced by the array of tools spread across the top of a bench across the room. More trinkets. An anvil-like vise was clamped to one side. Against another wall stood a furnace. There were two points of entry. One came from an opening in the wall, something like a ventilation shaft but with no screen, probably large enough for a person. It might have been instrumental in transporting him here. The other entrance was a door, undoubtedly locked. It might have been susceptible to one of the heftier trinkets available in the room, such as a steel mallet straight out of an abattoir, but his hands had been cinched with zip ties that were in turn roped to more zip ties which bound his feet together. He also was not alone.

In the middle of the room was the centerpiece, the goddess herself. Or so she had seemed yesterday (?) when he had witnessed her entrance to the hotel. Now she looked unmistakably mortal and vulnerable, bound to a chair. She wore an elegant silken cream dress, which played in stark contrast to the eyes alight with terror, face streaked with tears and a not so godly effluvium from her nostrils. She locked her gaze with Pawel's briefly, the solidarity of captivity, but then her attention was commanded by the other presence in the room.

Henry stepped around her. In the harsh glare of the lights, there should not have been a shadow on his face, but there seemed to be one all the same, like some kind of darkness he carried with him. He could have been an actor slipping through a curtain to emerge within a spotlight, but Pawel knew this was the real version of Henry. The difference was an absence. Whatever semblance of normal humanity he affected in his public persona was nonexistent here. He was a vacuum into which all light in the room should have vanished.

He approached Pawel with his hands behind him. Judging by the goddess's fixed expression on his back, they weren't empty.

'Oh, Pawel,' he chided. 'We are going to miss you in the kitchen.' He smiled but it held no warmth; it was a death's head with flesh.

Pawel felt a thousand tiny hooks scraping up his spine, leaving behind stipples of gooseflesh. He wasn't sure he'd be able to speak, but in a miniscule approximation of his usual voice, he managed to at least say, 'Mr. Henry, I...' before he trailed off, overwhelmed by the enormity of his situation. He looked to the goddess, as if she could offer some clue on how to progress or he could somehow draw strength from her.

She seemed to pick up on it because she screamed, an ear-splitting level the opposite of his own defeated croak. Pawel jerked up straight, but Henry barely reacted.

'You know, you should probably save that up for later,' he advised. He raised his voice a little but didn't bother to turn around. 'You'll have a lot more to scream about, and no one's going to hear it anyway. We might as well be on another planet in here. And the only god who can set you free...' Henry crouched in front of Pawel and brought his hands in front so he could show what he'd been hiding. '...has no interest in doing so.'

Pawel knew the object well, had used one like it many times in the kitchen. It had in fact been brought over from the laundry because its equal was allegedly stolen by another worker named Adam. Adam was never seen again by anyone. Disappeared in the night for parts unknown as if he'd stolen millions of dollars rather than a battery-operated carving knife. Pawel would be willing to bet this was the 'stolen' carving knife and the parts unknown had been arms, legs, and a torso incinerated in the furnace.

Henry held the knife up and revved it. The serrated blades shifted in their grinding enthusiasm. The knife was at least eight inches long. His friend Mikhail had sometimes held it in front of his crotch as he carved through slabs of meat, exaggerated ecstasy on his face. Something that was funny the first four or five times, much less so around the seventy-fifth. The ecstasy on Henry's face looked far more genuine.

Pawel's heels skidded on the floor as he pushed back against the wall, trying to find some phantom exit away from the reach of the knife.

'I can pay you!' the goddess shouted over the whirring.

Henry relinquished the switch and the blades settled. He turned to her, the knife still uncomfortably close to Pawel's face. He reflexively reached up to try to pry it away, but there was little slack. His hands could not even get as high as neck level.

'And will you pay for him too?' Henry jabbed the knife at Pawel, who turned his head in profile for a few more inches of clearance.

'Yes!' The goddess nodded, practically bouncing in the chair. Pawel's eyes filled with tears of gratitude.

Henry walked back to her. 'Interesting. And then what? You'll both just pretend you had never been here?'

'You haven't hurt us,' she said. 'We haven't seen you do anything.'

Pawel joined her with the effusive nodding. 'We have seen you do nothing!'

And just like that, Henry and the blade were in his face again. 'I've seen you, though. Would you like to tell the lady who just offered to spare your life why you were in her room?'

He and Mikhail happened to see her arrival. There was a constant flow of distinguished guests but to the staff their comings and goings may as well have been repairs on a space station, a world away. A confluence of events allowed him and Mikhail to emerge from the kitchen area for a bathroom break (anything else being heavily discouraged by Henry, of course) at just the right moment. The light from the world outside seemed to follow her through the lobby, the bejeweled wonder in impossibly sharp detail to Pawel's captive gaze. Her blonde hair was immaculately styled, braided into something like a crown around her head and intricately woven within the crown into a shape that spilled past its rim to her shoulders. She wore an aqua blue dress which barely shifted in her approach to the front desk, as if she glided above the carpet. She sparkled with tiny flashes of lightning from her earrings and rings, and the diamonds of a necklace encircling her throat. A finely sculpted face and figure, an oasis in the desert of Pawel's otherwise joyless life of hotel tedium and second class citizenry.

He came crashing back to reality when Mikhail nudged him and held his hands up in front of his chest as if he were palming two basketballs. He shook them to simulate a pair of massive breasts. *Some trinkets she is having, correct?* He usually didn't bother with English, and for good cause.

The whole thing might have ended there, but on their way back from the bathroom she mesmerized him all over again (the rear view was equally exceptional) and he overheard the room number when they gave her the key.

Pawel had learned quite a bit about locks back home.

While he'd been on his best behavior in the past month because of Henry's zero tolerance policy toward staff, Mikhail was right—they were some trinkets. There had been no answer when he snuck off and knocked later that evening and so he went in, certain no one was watching.

Henry watched him expectantly now, having somehow diverted the biggest secret in the room from his own to Pawel's. When there was no answer forthcoming, he thrust his hand into the pocket of Pawel's pants and easily extracted what was inside. Pawel groaned miserably as Henry took it over to the goddess.

'Can you identify these?'

Her eyes popped for an instant and she gave Pawel a withering look. She may not have been a true goddess, but he grew infinitely smaller anyway. Henry set the knife down and knelt to better present the offering of fabric. He unfolded her panties, the same shade of aqua blue as the dress she had worn yesterday. Within were the earrings and a couple of rings. They had been simple enough to get from the room safe, but the necklace wasn't to be found. Henry had probably taken it when he'd taken her.

'I can't be sure he didn't put them on at some point,' Henry said, almost apologetically. 'I sure wouldn't want to hold them under a black light to find out. We'd probably be better off just throwing them in the furnace.'

Pawel tried to block out the conversation. Henry's back was turned and the knife was free on the ground, maybe twelve feet away. Pawel attempted to stand, deciding it would be too difficult to crawl over to claim the knife without alerting Henry. Standing wasn't a much better option. He was awkwardly hunched over from the zip ties, and there was not enough give for him to move without jumping from place to place.

'He's trying to get up!' the goddess said.

Although Henry turned without any urgency and may have known anyway, Pawel's terror was nearly engulfed by a surge of anger. He'd been trying to save them both, for Christ's sake.

He took his seat against the wall again.

'I'll pay you...just let me go and you can keep him.'

'So you don't care what happens to him?'

'No! He's a disgusting pervert and a thief! Just let me go...I'll never tell anyone, I swear to God! And I'll...I'll do anything you want.'

Pawel saw his only out. She had everything to offer in the way of material gain but Henry would be an idiot to believe her and they were both going to die, unless...

'I will help you, Mr. Henry,' he said, a sick feeling settling into his stomach because if an opportunity didn't present itself for him to play the hero, he would be committed to the offer. 'I help you, I can't tell.'

The goddess launched into some rather unholy profanities, many beyond the scope of Pawel's grasp of the English language. 'Bastard cocksucker' did manage to register.

Henry ignored her outburst. 'You will? Why?'

Pawel sensed *to save myself* wasn't going to be a good enough answer, so he pointed to the goddess in the chair and said, 'She is fake.'

Henry looked at her as if truly appraising her for the first time. 'I don't know. She doesn't seem so fake to me.' He grabbed one of her breasts. She gamely tried not to react to affect her promise of cooperation, but fresh tears brimmed. 'That feels real enough.'

The sickness filled Pawel, one he could scarcely imagine living with, but at least he *might* live. So he insisted, 'Fake.'

'I suppose there's one way to settle this.' Henry released her breast, set the aqua blue underwear off to the side of the room and reclaimed the carving knife. The blades revved again. He drew them through the neckline of her dress as she screamed and struggled in the chair. The spotless cream soon displayed hundreds of bloody dots and smears. After a moment, both sides of the cream garment slipped away to either side, along with the cups of a bra. Pawel saw red droplets within the cups as Henry stepped aside, trickling over the edges. Her wounds were mostly incidental, as he had only wanted to cut away her dress, but there were gouges in the landscape of her bare flesh, scarlet trails running between the valley of her cleavage.

Henry looked at her like an ice sculptor planning his next cuts. Her breasts were bloodied from the spray of ground flesh. They stood firm without the support of her wardrobe, although heaving with the exertion of her pain. A bright sheen of blood fanned across the top of her chest. Pawel could even see the overhead lights reflected in it. Her screams harmonized with the carving knife. Henry's decision made, he brought the blade down the side of her right breast and burrowed in. It seemed improper for the sounds of slicing to be no different from the turkey, ham, and roast Pawel cut up in the kitchen, but they weren't. Visually, of course, it was something else entirely. Blood burst in vibrant crimson from the trench as Henry sawed across the meat of her breast. Every couple of seconds there would be another, a mini fire-work of exploding red.

Henry worked through the right breast and continued into the left. There was a brief couple of seconds where it was just the natural sound of the whirring blade, and then once again came the wet sounds of sharp metal easily clawing a path through tender skin and unresisting fat. More bursts of blood blew left and right past Henry, like sparks from a welder's torch. He eclipsed most of the horror as he carved. Her legs strained at the bonds where Pawel could see. The screams had taken on a wailing pitch, from something throaty and raw to a piercing whistle that set Pawel's teeth on edge. As Henry completed the incision, her cries trailed off and her legs slackened. He stepped aside to unveil his progress.

Pawel gawked with mouth agape at the macabre results. The mounds of both breasts slumped over, laying against her belly now, the majority detached from her chest. They depended from the remaining attachments of the lower portions of her breasts like inverted gumdrops stuffed with dissected flesh. Syrupy trails dribbled from the gaping cavities of her chest, her torso adorned with spatters and streams of flowing red. The cones of her breasts lifted once, pushed by tortured respiration, and then settled. The goddess stared back at Pawel with glassy eyes.

Henry cupped one of the breasts and crushed it in his hand. Moist, serrated layers of red and yellow tissue squeezed out like ground chuck, with minced and diced fragments which pooled in her lap as they draped over the jagged brims. The breast oozed clumps of white fat like the innards of manicotti.

'As you can see from my handiwork,' Henry said, 'not a drop of silicone.'

Pawel didn't understand most of the sentence, barely heard the words to begin with. He thought of Mikhail with his palms in front of his chest, marveling over the goddess's trinkets. Pawel turned away and vomited on the floor beside him. He couldn't remember when he last ate but whatever it was unfortunately reminded him of what he had just seen by way of color and texture, and he soon added to its volume.

'I think she would have paid,' Henry mused. 'She might have even kept her mouth shut. You, on the other hand…you claimed you could help me do her, but you can't even look at a little papercut without puking your guts out. I think we know who the fake is in here.'

Pawel closed his eyes against both his emesis and to insure he didn't look at the chair again, but they snapped open at the restarting of the carving knife. He found Henry approaching him with the blade held out like a magic wand angled toward Pawel's crotch.

'It's not too late,' Henry shouted over the blades. 'You can at least still fuck her.'

Instinct took over, however unwise. Pawel moved to block the knife with his hands. With better planning he might have maneuvered the zip tie into the blade to free up his hands, but instead he offered them to the knife with the universal sign language for 'stop.' Searing agony ignited as it sawed deep between the middle and ring finger of the nearest hand—the right— and continued to deepen the trench past knuckles and into the palm. Somehow he could not stop hearing the sounds despite the deafening screams he summoned in his torment, the bones in his hand resisting but ultimately succumbing to the scourge of throttling stainless steel, thousands of blood droplets blasted into his face. One eye squeezed shut from the spray, but the other dutifully watched as the space between the middle and ring finger expanded to the original distance between the pinkie and index.

Pawel at last managed to wrest his hand away, now something more akin to a lobster claw.

He must have passed out as time played a strange trick between one blink and the next. One minute he urged himself to fend off Henry as the carving knife resumed its original trajectory, then blinked and found his pants cut away, new wounds scorching his thighs and abdomen. The heavy patter of red droplets beneath the divot in his hand had grown to a puddle thick enough to see his reflection. The humiliation of having his genitals exposed restored a fading part of his consciousness, one that noted the silence of the carving knife roughly half a second before it roared to life again and ate into the skin of his groin. He thought he might have been screamed out by that point, but not so. A new agony resurrected all the pain centers of his body, live wires alight.

Henry worked the blade against his scrotum, the tender skin exploding at the touch of its teeth, blasting crimson jets across Pawel's thighs and up his belly and chest. The carving knife worked its way behind Pawel's scrotum, making a neat circumnavigation to the other side while sparing his testicles and penis until with a flick of his wrist it found its way through the other side and Pawel's scrotal pouch dropped away from between his legs like a soaked sponge. Excruciating molten pain flared through the empty space. His jerked about as if hooked up to a car battery. He looked at the grisly point of excavation, unable to comprehend, even as he shrieked. The madness of the scene became even more obscure as Henry withdrew the scrotal pouch from between Pawel's legs, the dick dead and slumped over. Pawel saw a brief glimpse of the underside, the sacs within like miniature brains where the furrows were fashioned from infected-looking tendrils. Henry worked the knife around to his liking until the tip slid within the length of Pawel's estranged penis and the girth clamped tight over the blade with a wet sound. Henry held the knife aloft where the cock held fast to the end of the blade like a bizarre flag. The testicles dropped from the pouch at the ends of their cords.

'I'm still counting on you to join in,' Henry said. With that, he made his way back over to the chair with the goddess, where he fussed with the goddess's dress.

Blink.

Time travel tricks again. Pawel came back to find Henry crouched at the chair, the gown drawn aside, the goddess's sex revealed and bloodied now from the rolling crimson tributaries of the mutilation above. Henry raised the knife again, Pawel's organ still a makeshift accessory. Pawel tried to will himself back to oblivion—the life he would have committed the vilest of acts to sustain, now something he'd gladly relinquish for a release from this hell.

Blink.

But no time passed. Henry worked the pocket of excised genitalia between the goddess's vaginal lips and slid it back and forth with the handle of the knife. He did not turn it on, allowing the distinct audibility of this awful congress; Pawel's cock, twelve feet away from his crotch, slipping between the membranes of the goddess's lifeless, cooling cunt, back and forth, with his balls pendulum-like, evicted from the pouch that had faithfully held them for almost thirty years before today. There was something somehow *larval* about the noise; with each insertion, Pawel imagined a tumbleweed of maggots laying waste a rotting cadaver.

Blink.

Still alive, somehow.

Henry above him again, the carving knife still ornamented with Pawel's genitals. Pawel opened his mouth to say something, unsure what, and Henry plunged the blade between his lips, the entirety of his scrotum lodged on his tongue. His testicles slid across his face, the strands of their cords like stretched bubblegum on his lower lip. The blades revved in his mouth, his genitals the harness for an instant meat grinder which tore through the frail skin. The viscera of his sexual anatomy exploded around the saw in a whirlwind of chunks that expelled through his lips like the remnants from a woodchipper. His tongue hit the blade, forked and then sliced in half. It scored the roof of his mouth, the uvula. Blood and genital debris filled his throat in a jagged stream, clogging his airway. His lips shredded as Henry withdrew the knife, its roar filling the world once more. The last adherent scrotal pieces on the blade tore themselves into hundreds and thousands of tinier fragments, scattering through the air in a tornado to wash over Pawel in a baptism of mutilation confetti.

Blink.

Too Many Cooks
by
Armand Rosamilia

His name was Jonathan and he spoke with a slight Chicago accent. He'd told Henry he was a runaway and had been living on the streets half his life. At nearly thirty he looked the part: hard eyes and rough hands. Luckily for Henry he was a slight man, who looked like he hadn't had a good meal in far too long.

A hot bowl of soup, a warm bed and the vague promise of a job had enticed Jonathan to stay at the hotel. He'd watched the front desk for the occasional tourist, rare this time of season. It allowed Henry to do some repairs in the rest of the hotel and prepare a few more elaborate traps for future guests. Sometimes he thought the act of butchering people was only a small part of what he did. The fun was in the planning.

It's not the kill, it's the thrill of the chase, Henry often thought.

Jonathan had done what he was told. He'd often slept in the office with a book in hand, needing nothing more than a drink of water. He never strayed too far from the lobby and Henry had finally asked if he stayed in the room he'd been offered.

'No, sir… I prefer to sleep in a chair. It's a definite step up from sleeping on the ground. All I need is some light to read by and I can fall asleep anywhere,' Jonathan had said.

Jonathan had a weathered backpack he kept close at all times. He often rifled through it but usually pulled out a paperback. Whenever Henry came through the lobby Jonathan would shove a book under the counter and smile, as if he hadn't been reading.

Henry didn't care if he read because when someone came into the hotel he was his absolute best, pleasant and smiling as he checked them in. He'd promptly ring Henry and not go back to reading until he was alone again.

The days turned into weeks and Henry sometimes forgot Jonathan was in the building. The man was quiet. He only asked to leave the hotel once or twice a week and was usually back within an hour or two. Usually just before midnight, which made Henry curious. He never left his backpack behind but Henry had glimpsed inside enough to know he had two more changes of clothing, a toothbrush, deodorant and over a dozen books.

'Where do you go on your weekly pilgrimages into town?' Henry asked casually one night, right before he knew Jonathan was going to excuse himself and disappear.

Jonathan looked like a deer caught in headlights but recovered with a fake smile. 'I go and see some of the people I used to hang out with. Old friends. Catch up on old times. That's it.'

Henry didn't believe him but said nothing. Instead, he wished Jonathan a good night and said he was going to retire early unless someone wandered in for a room.

Jonathan got a three minute head-start out the door before Henry donned a dark coat and cap, pulled low so you couldn't see his face. He followed in the direction Jonathan had gone and soon found himself in a worse part of town than his hotel was in.

The area was filthy with homeless. Henry made a mental note to come and visit during the daylight hours, bearing smiles and food and a promise to shelter some of them during the cold months. He could test out a few new theories he had about the lengths he could go with torturing someone.

Jonathan was seated on a stoop under a yellowed light, reading a book.

Did he come out to this godforsaken area to read? Did he read all the time? Henry blended into the shadows.

Henry shifted back and forth on his heels as he watched Jonathan, wondering what the man was doing besides reading. He could do this back at the hotel. Was he really only coming out for this? Maybe he liked this spot. Maybe this was where he'd lived before the hotel.

A couple, a man and a woman who looked like vagrants, came down the sidewalk but quickly crossed the street before getting to Jonathan. Both eyed him warily.

Jonathan glanced at them and smiled before going back to his paperback.

After nearly two hours Jonathan put his paperback back in his bag and walked slowly back to the hotel, Henry staying ahead of him.

Now Henry was truly curious about his new hire.

*

Henry smiled at the couple checking in, chatting about the weather and how their vacation was going so far.

Jonathan began to walk to the office now that his work was done and Henry would be taking over to deliver them to their room.

'You know what... I have an idea, Jonathan,' Henry said, calling the man back. 'I'm going to switch their room and I'd like you to walk them to the top suite.'

The woman looked nervous. 'Uh, that's fine. We're on a shoestring budget. The room you have offered us is perfect. We don't want to trouble you and an upgrade sounds like more money.'

'Don't be silly. There's no extra charge at all. In fact, I'll even take twenty off your bill when you check out. How does that sound?' Henry asked and smiled. He handed Jonathan the key to the room.

'You want me to walk them to the room?' Jonathan asked. This was unprecedented on Henry's part. *He* was the one who took the guests to the room. No one else.

'You've earned it,' Henry said. 'You're the best employee I've ever hired. I want you to grow as an employee and as a person. I'm here for you, Jonathan. And - to start this... More responsibility.' He smiled. 'And, with that, will come a pay-rise.' He laughed. 'More money for more books.'

It looked like the man was about to cry. He stared at the key in his hand. It wasn't just a key to the couple's room. It was a symbol to progression.

'They're waiting,' Henry leaned in and whispered with the biggest smile he could muster.

As soon as Jonathan was gone, leading the couple to the upper floor of the hotel and the furthest room from the front desk, Henry went into the office and searched for the backpack Jonathan carried. At first he couldn't see it but after a quick search he saw it tucked behind the filing cabinet.

Henry opened the backpack and frowned. It was packed with paperbacks and larger volumes of books. Not much else.

He was just about to close it up and stuff it back where he'd found it when he read a title.

Twentieth Century Serial Killers.

Henry pulled another book. It was a biography of Bundy.

Another book about Dahmer.

Lucas.

Gacey.

Jonathan was reading nothing but serial killer books.

*

Henry followed Jonathan once a week for the next month before he gave up. All Jonathan had done was to sit on the stoop, reading his books, and smiling at passersby.

A police officer had come into the hotel just after midnight when Henry was manning the front desk. He looked like a man on a mission.

'Can I help you, officer?' Henry asked. He glanced out of the lobby, hoping not to see a squad of officers, ready to charge into the hotel and shut him down.

'Do you have a gentleman who works for you name of Jonathan?' The officer asked.

Henry acted like he was thinking. What had Jonathan done or what had he told the police? Had he figured out what Henry was up to? So many questions.

'Sir, I asked you a question,' the cop said.

'I'm sorry. Yes. Of course. The poor man has been helping me upfront most days. Why… did something happen to him?' Henry asked.

'He's wanted in connection with a homicide,' the cop said, staring intently at Henry.

It was an uncomfortable look. Henry tried to relax, putting on a shocked look and covering his mouth for effect. 'Homicide? As in you think Jonathan killed someone?'

The police officer nodded.

'Horrible. Maybe it was self-defense? I've only known him a short time. So tragic. Where did this happen? I know he liked to visit old friends each week when he wasn't working,' Henry said.

'Jonathan targeted several of the homeless. We're piecing it together but it looks like, over the course of a few months, he's killed men and women…' The officer looked uncomfortable. He sighed. 'Even children.'

'Dear God,' Henry said, hoping he wasn't laying it on too thick. He wasn't shocked. He was pissed. The man had been out killing people in public. This would not be good for business, for the hotel or for Henry to continue his own fun.

'Any idea where he could be? Did he leave something behind in his room?'

Henry shook his head. The last thing he needed was for the police to search the hotel.

If push comes to shove I could perhaps blame Jonathan for everything, Henry thought but dismissed it. A cursory check would reveal how long Henry's fun had been going on, long before Jonathan had arrived.

'He actually slept in my office. I know it sounds odd but Jonathan was an odd sort of person. Not in a bad way. He had everything in an old backpack he kept with him at all times,' Henry said.

'We recovered the backpack. Filled with filth about serial killers. Smut fiction from deranged authors,' the cop said. 'Mind if we look in your office? Perhaps he left something behind.'

'Feel free,' Henry said, hoping he hadn't left anything incriminating himself. He tried to relax… The office was empty of anything like that and had been since Jonathan had been employed there.

*

Two nights later Jonathan arrived in the hotel lobby looking like he'd originally appeared: dirty and looking disturbed.

'Henry, I know you don't have to help me but I could really use it. I didn't do the things they're saying I did. I swear,' Jonathan said.

'If you didn't, who did? I know I didn't,' Henry said as a joke, amusing himself.

'Let me hide in one of the rooms. I know you don't owe me anything but I had nowhere else to turn,' Jonathan said. He looked so miserable.

'How did you escape from the authorities?'

'I… I'd rather not say.' Jonathan kept glancing at the hotel door.

'If you tell me everything I'll hide you, but I want nothing but the truth,' Henry said. An accomplice, maybe? Someone to help him when the going gets tough? Someone to turn into a patsy if things turn to shit…

'Fair enough.' Jonathan smiled. 'Thank you.'

'Don't thank me yet. If I sense you're lying I will call the police and hand you over myself. There is nothing worse in this world than a liar,' Henry said and led Jonathan down the hall to one of the rooms you couldn't open from the inside. He knew he couldn't use Jonathan. The passing thought about training him to help him out with the darker hobbies... A passing fancy. It would never work. Besides... This was going to be fun.

*

The room was sparse with only a bed and a single wooden chair in the corner.

Henry snuck in and watched Jonathan sleep, snoring softly. He pulled the manacles from underneath the bed slowly, making sure they didn't jingle and ruin the surprise.

He managed to snap Jonathan's left wrist and left ankle before he stirred.

'Good morning. How did you sleep?' Henry asked, rushing around to the other side of the bed and getting the other ankle in place before Jonathan was fully awake and struggling to get out of his predicament.

'What are you doing? I thought you were going to help me.'

'Oh, I am. I just want to make sure you're not distracted. I want to have your undivided attention, too. Now... tell me everything. I'll get the other handcuff on you shortly,' Henry said.

'I don't think so,' Jonathan said angrily but his eyes went wide when he noticed the taser in Henry's hand.

'I think so.' Henry smiled. 'Here's how this will work. I want to know everyone you've managed to kill and how you've managed to kill them. I want specific details. I don't care about the why. That's of no interest to me. We all have our ticks and quirks, right? I know why I do what I do and it's only my business. I respect a man's privacy.'

'You're nuts if you think I'll confess to you. I thought you were different. I thought maybe I could trust you,' Jonathan said.

'Why in the world would you think that?'

Jonathan sighed and stopped struggling. 'I don't really know. I just got a good vibe from you. I hardly ever get it. I thought we had a good thing going. I helped you at the hotel, which gave me a nice close base so I could take care of the homeless problem in the city. Those rats and scumbags used to steal from me. Beat me. Do... other things to me. I wanted to pay them all back.'

'Again... your motivation is your business. I want to know the *how* of it all. After that I have a big decision to make,' Henry said.

'Whether to let me go or turn me in?'

Henry smiled. 'No. Whether to torture you for hours or release you and accept you as a willing partner in my hotel. You see, Jonathan, I have my own stories to tell. It's been so lonely keeping all of this greatness hidden away.' Maybe he could use him? He walked around to the side of the bed and pulled out the handcuff. 'Allow me to slip this on or I will taser you first and then do it. Up to you.'

Jonathan reluctantly let Henry put the manacle on his wrist.

'Now, I'm going to have a seat and I want to hear all about your killings. Make it interesting, too. You're literally bargaining for me to release you,' Henry said.

*

Henry waved at the last piece of Jonathan tossed into the furnace.

In the end, he'd decided too many cooks in the kitchen wasn't a good thing. While Jonathan's stories had been fascinating, and at one point Henry had paused the man to get them both something to drink and a pad and pen to take notes, he'd seen too much hunger in Jonathan's eyes.

The man was dangerous and not in a good way.

Henry had no doubt they could have had some wild and crazy nights and days together, working in tandem in the comfort of the hotel.

But he didn't want to have to sleep with one eye open.

PRESENT DAY

Agata
by
Matt Shaw

I was still smiling when Agata turned to me with a look of confusion etched on her otherwise pretty face.

'I don't understand,' she said. 'Where is the hot tub? Where's the television set?' She turned away from me and scanned the cellar for a second time, perhaps curious as to whether she had missed a doorway to another room. She hadn't. This was it. This was all there was. The last room she gets to see before she dies.

'What's the matter?' I asked her, despite knowing full well what the answer was. 'You don't like it?'

'I'm confused,' she said. Words not needed as her confusion was still evident from the expression on her face.

'Did you want to look around?' I asked her.

She scanned the room again.

'There's nothing to see,' she said, still confused.

'What, are you joking? There's loads to see.'

'You're scaring me.'

I looked at her. Now it was my turn to be confused. How was I scaring her? She hadn't seen the other side of me yet. At the moment, I thought I was being quite pleasant.

'I want to go back upstairs.' She moved towards the stairs that led the way back to the cellar door and the foyer. I blocked her path and grabbed her by the arm. She let out a little whimper as I increased the pressure with which I grasped her. 'You're hurting me.'

'You're not going anywhere,' I told her. 'I offered to show you around. It's polite to say, oh I don't know, *yes please* when someone offers to show you around so - how's about it? Do you want to look around?'

Her eyes were already welling up. Funny. I haven't even started to try and upset her yet.

'Yes please,' she said quietly.

'Sorry? I can't hear you.'

'Yes please!'

'Yes please what?'

'I'd love for you to show me around!'

'That's better!' I laughed. 'I would *love* to show you around. All you had to do was ask! Come. It'll be my pleasure.'

I dragged her towards the workstation first where the tools hung. She didn't try pulling against my strong grip.

'This is where I keep my tools,' I told her.

Hammers, hacksaws, a rusting chainsaw powered by petrol, a set of garden shears, various thicknesses of ropes and bindings, bamboo canes, pliers, a car battery, bricks, a vice, a blow-torch, sledge-hammer, drugs - both prescription and illegal, knives (both kitchen and hunting).... Other bits and pieces buried under the obvious.

'These are what I'm likely to use to kill you,' I told her.

She turned to me. Eyes wide. Panic. 'What?!'

'I mean - not all of them but... There'll be something there I'll want to use.'

She started pulling against my grip. If I'm not careful, she'll manage to rip herself free so... I quietened her down with a right hook to the face. She fell to the floor like a sack of shit, clearly stunned. Her cheek, where my fist connected, immediately red. Tomorrow, if she were to be alive, it would most likely be black.

'You know,' I said as I picked her up off the floor, 'I actually liked you. I mean, a lot. Had it not been for the fact I'm incapable of love... I reckon we could have had a future together. You were obedient. You were pretty... You know how many times I masturbated thinking about you? Wondering what your hand would feel like around my prick or how warm the inside of your snatch was as I pushed inside you?' I sighed. 'You had to fucking ruin it, didn't you? You had to be a nosey little cunt and fuck things up...' I pulled her towards the furnace. With every other step, she stumbled over her own feet. Still dazed. 'Well - bet you regret that now, huh?' She was trying to say something over and over. Hazard a guess, it would be something along the lines of being sorry or begging me not to hurt her. If she wanted me to pay attention, she shouldn't mumble. 'This,' I said as we reached the far end of the cellar, 'is the furnace. This is where I'll be disposing of your body when I'm through with it.' She struggled again and was - for a second time - quietened down with a punch, to the gut this time. Her body wrapped itself round my clenched fist as she gasped for air. When I pulled my hand away, and released my grip of her arm, she slumped to the hard floor wheezing.

Knowing she wasn't going anywhere in a hurry, I walked over to the workstation and lifted the heavy sledgehammer from where it laid on it's side. With it gripped firmly in both hands, I casually strolled back to where Agata was still struggling for air. She hadn't even noticed what I was doing.

No words needed, I lifted the sledgehammer high in the air before bringing it crashing down on her left leg first. The bone shattered and crunched beneath the weight of the sledgehammer. Her screamed echoed through the cellar and was promptly followed by cries of pain and - then - another scream as I destroyed the bone in her right leg. Seconds later and the screaming drifted to nothing as she blacked out from the pain. I tried to not let the disappointment get to me at the fact she had passed out so quickly with the thought that - with her out cold - I have more time to plan my next move.

I can really enjoy this. Really take my time.

It wasn't as though I had had much fun with the guest earlier. I mean, sure, there had been *some* fun to be had, there always is - no matter how brief our time together. It's just - it's much more fun when it lasts for longer and once his cock had been cut off, he was pretty much done with shock stealing his consciousness.

I looked back down to Agata. This definitely won't be quick. I'm going to take my time. And I'm going to make sure that she'll feel everything. I tossed the sledgehammer to one side and didn't bat an eyelid as it noisily clattered to the floor. In my head I was no longer in the room. In my head, I was playing through all that I was quickly planning.

'You rest up, girl.' I said, 'We have such sights to show you.' I laughed at my feeble impression of Clive Barker's *Pinhead* character from his *Hellraiser* books. The voice might have been a million miles from the spoken words shown in the classic horror film but - one thing is for sure... Pinhead is a fucking pussy compared to me.

This is going to be fun.

*

Agata slowly opened her watery eyes. I watched as she struggled to focus on her surroundings. I watched as she focused on me. I watched as the panic set in when she realised that what had happened hadn't been a bad dream. It was all very, very real.

'How's the pain?' I asked her.

She whispered meekly, 'I can't feel anything.'

'Good.'

I had injected her with a spinal block to take away the pain. A quick little injection which numbs the area downwards from point of needle insertion. The state of her legs, I wasn't entirely sure it was going to help but - evidently - it at least took the edge off for her making it a little more bearable. This isn't me being nice. This is me not wishing for her to be distracted by the pain that is coming.

Leaving her where she lay on the floor, I walked over to the workstation and started scanning across the various tools of destruction. All that time, whilst she had slept, I had had ample opportunity to decide on what to do to her and I have a million and one ideas but - I hadn't given any thought as to where I should start.

I looked over my shoulder, back to Agata. She was so doped up she wasn't even trying to move. In fact, she even looked a little sleepy - probably due to what I had put her body through.

'Don't you go falling asleep on me,' I said.

'I want to go home,' she whispered.

Home as in upstairs to the sleeping quarters or home as in back to her own country, I wondered. Not that it makes any difference as to which. She isn't going anywhere just yet, and when she does finally get to move - it'll only be across to the furnace.

'You know - when I first met you... When you walked into my office for your interview... I actually fancied you. In my head, if only for a split second, I even imagined having a relationship with you.' I paused a moment as I thought back to when it had happened. 'You know, I think that was the first time such thoughts have ever popped into my head. Normally when I see someone, my first thought is wondering what their head will look like on a stick.' I laughed. 'Question,' I needed to talk to her directly to stop her from sleeping. Maybe I had used too much anaesthetic? 'Did you feel the same towards me? Did you see me and imagine a happy future with me? Perhaps thinking of the two of us walking hand in hand down the road? Maybe a trip to the cinema, feeding each other popcorn? Or maybe you just thought about us fucking. You on your back, me on top - just fucking pounding you as you scream for it harder and faster. Is that what happened?' I reached for the blow-torch. Never been used before. 'Did you feel a burning in your loins for me?'

I walked back over to where she lay. She was staring at the ceiling. With my spare hand I clicked my fingers above her face until she focused on me.

'Well?' I pushed for an answer. 'Did you feel a burning in your loins?'

She struggled to remain focused on me. She's away with the fairies. Probably doesn't even know that she is naked. Probably doesn't even know that I am too. That would be the roofie I had slipped her earlier - another way to make this that little bit easier for me.

Her body is as perfect as I had imagined it to be, with the exception of her legs. They're fucked now, there's no coming away from that. Her face is beautiful despite the faraway look in her eyes and the streaked make-up from where she'd been crying earlier. Her stomach is flat. To the right of her belly button, there's a small scar. If I had to hazard a guess, I would presume it to be from an appendix being removed. Her chest. Her breasts are slightly more than a handful with the smallest of nipples. Erect. Side effect of the drugs? Not exactly cold down here, given the furnace. Unless, even in her current state, she was aroused by my dirty talk planting the seed of us fucking. Couldn't blame her. Even I was semi-hard just from talking about fucking but then - I did have the images in my head too: My cock sliding into her tight, wet pussy…

Twitch.

Not wanting to get ahead and frustrating myself to the point where I couldn't wait to do anything but stick it in her, I carried on admiring her body. A neatly trimmed landing strip runs down to her vagina. Her cunt itself is neat with the slimmest of lips. Pretty pink. My mouth waters at the thought of running my tongue along her slit before pushing up and into her. The taste of her juices flowing over my tongue. Hell, a cunt that pretty - I wouldn't even give a fuck if she pissed on me.

Twitch.

Another look at her legs. Had she been surviving this, she'd definitely be in a wheelchair for the rest of her life. Had she been surviving...

I looked back at her cunt and kneeled down on the floor. Setting the blow-torch down next to me, I reached across to her gash and ran a finger down it. I couldn't help but lick my lips at the prospect of both tasting and penetrating it.

Erect.

'Well?' I asked. Leaving my hand in place, I focused back on her face. 'Did you think of us fucking? Did your loins burn with desire as a moistness dampened your knickers?'

She was looking at me but - going from her expression - I don't think she heard a word that I was saying. More to the point, I don't think she felt my finger running up and down her slit. Curious to know for sure, I pushed two fingers inside her - pushing against the friction caused by the dryness. She didn't register. I'd made the whole area too numb, obviously. But was it numb enough?

I picked the blow-torch up and fired it up - no pun intended. The flame started flicking a mixture of yellow and orange, a hint of blue, until I tweaked the setting and turned it to a roaring spit of blue and white. Looking from blow-torch to her face, she hadn't noticed. And, if she had, she didn't care.

'I'll be honest with you,' I said. 'I'm not entirely sure if this will hurt or not...' I shrugged as I aimed the flame down towards her cunt. With my eyes fixed on hers, to gauge any kind of reaction, I paused a moment. Still nothing. No begging me not to do it. No attempt at moving. She may as well have been a corpse. Not that it really bothers me. I looked at her pink pussy and - then - moved the flame closer until it touched flesh. Immediately the pinkness disappeared - replaced first with a dark, blistering brown and then with a blackness. The pubic hairs shrivelled and all but vanished in a waft of smoke. I pulled the flame back, not wanting to overcook it, and set the blow-torch down onto the floor. The smell of her cunt burning as it continued bubbling away was exquisite and I couldn't help myself but to lean down closer and breathe it all in. I hacked up some phlegm into the back of my mouth and then dribbled it down onto the crisped gash. Not only would it cool it down but it would also serve as a lubricant when I see how different it feels to fuck a burns victim.

'What's that smell?' she whispered.

It doesn't bother me that she can't feel it now because I know - when the drugs wear off - she'll feel it all then. I just need to make sure I keep her alive long enough to let the drugs wear off. Shouldn't be a problem. There's still much to do. There are lessons for her to learn and I really want to fuck her.

I hocked another mouthful of spit and phlegm down onto her cunt and tentatively ran it over her vagina with a cupped hand - worried that, despite the previous mouthful of bile, it could still be hot. Nope. At least - not on the outside. I pushed my fingers in, past the cracked burnt lips. The flames appeared to have not done any damage on the inside. At least, not deep inside where the tips of my fingers reached. The entry point was definitely a little crinkled to the touch.

I pulled my hand away and positioned myself over Agata's broken body. Her eyes fixed on mine but she had no idea what was to come - both figuratively and literally speaking.

I spat in my left hand and wiped it on my cock as I moved it closer to her waiting pussy. Without a word of warning to her, I closed my eyes as I guided myself into her lubricated orifice. To my disappointment, I couldn't feel much difference between sticking it in this cunt and one that hadn't been touched by fire. I guess the flame needs to go inside too? Regardless, she felt nice and tight - just as I had imagined and it *did* feel good, sliding back and forth. Maybe... I sighed. Maybe I can just do this for a while. I can always stop in a minute...

*

My cum was still dribbling out of her when I walked back over to her, bindings in hand along with a hacksaw. I had gotten carried away. Part of me was frustrated with myself as I hadn't fulfilled my plans. The other part of me didn't give a fuck. The orgasm had still been mind-blowing. For me at least. I'm pretty sure she hadn't felt the full Henry experience.

I dropped the hacksaw before lowering myself to my knees, still clutching the bindings. One at a time, I tied them to her wrists and ankles as a strong tourniquet.

Agata started to cry. I glanced at her face and saw an expression of pain and discomfort. I smiled. The medication was wearing off.

'Does it hurt?' I asked her. She was in too much pain to answer me. I didn't push her for a yes or no answer. There was no need. The look on her face and knowledge of what she had been through was enough. 'You only have yourself to blame,' I told her. 'You went snooping where you weren't invited. You knew the rules. Staff members stick to their areas and that's it.' I wasn't sure if she was listening to me as her cries had become louder as the full extent of the pain became obvious as the last of the medication continued to wear off. 'You touched things you shouldn't have touched. And just think - if you hadn't done - you'd still be upstairs right now, standing on the reception desk smiling sweetly to people coming and going...'

I paused a moment - not to let her think about what I had said but because I was suddenly very aware the front desk was unmanned. This was the first time I had been left in such a position - only me and one other running the place. What if someone had come in and was waiting? Just like that - I realised I didn't have as much time as I had initially hoped and - actually - I was already pushing my luck.

Fuck.

No need to be disappointed. I can always take a little more time with the next guest. Especially if I wait for a couple to come in. Someone to really sink my teeth into, figuratively speaking. Or - thinking as I go - maybe wait until I've employed more staff so I don't ever have to feel rushed again? My thoughts were distracted by Agata's screaming. Fair to say the meds had well and truly worn off now and she was feeling everything. *Good.* Just because I'm in a hurry now - it doesn't mean I don't want her to feel it.

Still kneeling down next to her, I collected the hacksaw from the floor and lined it up alongside her left wrist.

'I'm sorry, honey, we need to be quick. I have a hotel to run. Anyway - here's a lesson for you that you'll have no choice but to learn, it's just a shame you won't live long enough to put the lesson into practice. And what's the lesson you ask? *Don't touch what doesn't belong to you.*'

I started hacking backwards and forwards with the saw. The teeth dug into her flesh and ripped it open before continuing down through the stringy muscles and tendons before hitting bone. The change in material being cut suddenly sent small vibrations through the hand gripped to the handle - similar to what is experienced when cutting through wood. The noises, ripping flesh and biting teeth, were drowned out by her agonised screams.

*

I opened the cellar door having had a quick wash downstairs before putting my clothes back on. Agata was gone - burning away in the furnace - and I was alone. Or at least I had thought I was. A couple was standing at the reception desk, patiently waiting and giggling between themselves. I recognised the man from when he'd checked in yesterday. Duncan Bradshaw. If memory served correctly Agata had booked him in with no set date to leave due to work being done at his own home.

'Good evening, Mr. Bradshaw. Terribly sorry to have kept you waiting. A bit understaffed this evening...'

'That's fine. I was just letting you know that I've got a guest staying with me if that is okay?'

'We charge by the room, not the number of occupants.' I smiled. 'But thank you for letting me know.' I realised that the girl had a distinct lack of luggage with her and immediately wondered as to her hourly charge. Best not ask. Guests value their privacy. 'Will you be needing anything brought to the room? Bottle of wine, perhaps?'

Duncan looked at his date. She shook her head and said to him, 'I'm fine, thank you.'

Duncan relayed the message to me, 'We're good - thank you.'

'Well then,' I told them, 'I hope you have a pleasant evening.'

The couple smiled.

'You too,' Duncan said as he walked towards the elevators.

My eyes fixed on the woman's arse as they waited for the elevator to come and take them to their room. The damage I could do to that, given half a chance. I smiled to myself at the thought and promptly looked away when Duncan turned back to me - clearly curious to know if I was still there. I headed for my office with dark thoughts starting to formulate.

INTERVAL

I was sitting in my office with my feet up on the table. On the screen before me was not one of the usual evening movies playing but - instead - footage from each of the occupied rooms. Usually after I've indulged in my little hobby, I feel relaxed. Elevated. Almost happy. Not today though. Today I feel frustrated.

Agata had been one of my longest serving staff members. I'm not bummed about having to send her to the cellar. I'm annoyed that I didn't get to enjoy it as much as I should have. I just got carried away - going from one murder to another and I had been caught off guard, catching her in the office like that. In hindsight, I should have waited for the clock to strike 11pm. That's the time, as written at the entrance point, that the doors lock and guests have to press a buzzer if they wish to come in. A buzzer which can be heard from down in the cellar. Had I waited, I wouldn't have had to worry about people hanging around the reception area. I wouldn't have had to worry about them wandering off round the hotel, looking for someone to help them with their query or booking in. More importantly, I wouldn't have had to stress about them seeing something they shouldn't have.

I don't know. Maybe I should stop this little hobby until I have more staff. Easier said than done. If I'm not entertaining a guest I slip into a dark depression. My mood gets snappy and people notice a change in me that makes them feel uncomfortable. All the time I am enjoying my hobby, and I'm not in the process of indulging in its delights, I've found I can slip a metaphorical mask on. A little like Norman Bates, I guess - thinking back to *Psycho*. I can come across as charming and friendly....

Psycho?

Is that what I am?

Sudden movement from Duncan's room distracted me and I focused in on that part of the screen. They had gone from just standing there, talking, to kissing each other passionately. A whore that french kisses. His breath must be minty fresh. Usually, unless your mouth is in tip top condition, they decline such a service...

I reached to the keyboard and pressed a combination of keys to enlarge that section of the screen, blocking out the distractions from the other occupied rooms. I always like to watch when the guests get kinky with each other and yet I'm always disappointed when it proves vanilla. The girl lies on her back, legs apart. The man climbs on top. They have sex, he ejaculates. He rolls off and he goes to sleep. The woman cuddles in. It's boring. I want the sex toys to be brought into it. I want to watch the woman bang him with a strap-on. I want to watch the man choke the living shit out of the woman. I want to see her take it up the arse. Hell, I want to see her have him piss on her tits or her piss in his mouth. Maybe take a shit on his chest and rub it in with her breasts. If they're going to put on a porn show for me, I want the juicy stuff. Not the PG-13 crap. This isn't a Meg Ryan film. There's no Tom Hanks romance shit here.

Fuck, I'm showing my age.

The woman is stripping off on screen. The screen isn't the best of resolutions but she seems to have a nice enough body. I hope - if he is paying - it's not big money. She's not worth mega bucks. Unless, of course, she lets him piss on her. I'd go an extra twenty for that.

He's stripping off now. Okay, let's see what we're working with. To have a good porn show, you need a solid tool that's bigger than the average. You want the girl to take a painful pounding.

Shirt's off.

Pants are off.

Boxers down to ankles.

A mediocre erection. A little disappointing if I am to be honest but it's better than some I have seen. Shame it's not the guest from earlier, the one whacking off in his bedroom. That was a tool to be proud of. Hence why I put it in the fridge. Too impressive to chuck that out.

The girl is on her knees and her mouth is around the man's cock. She's probably hoping that - with a little encouragement - it might get a little bigger. I doubt it but God does love a trier.

Duncan is gripping the side of the mattress he is sitting on, clenching the sheets in his hands as he does so. He's pulling a funny face. Oh, fuck, don"t tell me he is about to blow his load already. Worst porno ever... In fact... I think they need some instruction; a little help to make the best porn film possible.

I glanced up at the clock hanging on the wall. It's 11pm. The front doors are locked. No more visitors coming in. Given how disappointed I feel about wasting Agata, I don't see the harm in going up there and helping them out. Show them how to really put a show on for the camera.

In fact...

I pressed the *escape* key on the keyboard and the previous screen was displayed showing the other rooms. A quick scan of the other rooms, and the corridors… No one is walking around. They're all in their rooms - good little guests and *now*…

Another button press. All the doors locked.

Now they'll never leave again.

First things first though… I need to teach Duncan and his woman the way to put on a real show. Then, when I am done with them, I've got the whole night to work the other rooms too. Time to close this hotel down for a while so I can concentrate on getting staff again. There's enough savings, both mine and stolen from guests, to tide me over for a couple of months. Could always hold a relaunch party when I'm fully staffed again. Might even let those guests survive the night.

Stop.

Getting ahead of myself. Don't rush. Don't make the same mistake I made with Agata. Take my time with this. Enjoy my last night of some serious indulgence.

I stood up and walked to the cupboard at the far side of the room. I opened it up. Various files, piles of unsorted paperwork… None of which I want. There, on the top shelf… The camera. Next to that? The tripod.

I always wanted to make a movie.

Matt Shaw

Part Four

THE
OTHER
GUESTS

(IN NO PARTICULAR ORDER)

Room 27
by
Kealan Patrick Burke

The lights in the hotel lobby flicker as Desmond steps in out of the rain. Shaking himself like a dog, he adjusts his spectacles, sparing a moment to clear them of the fog, and squints at his surroundings. He does not have a reservation, but this is typical of Desmond. He has never booked anything in his life: not a meal, or a cruise, or a flight. He has never operated on a schedule and the liberation that has afforded him has made his seventy-eight years on this earth rather pleasurable. He has, in every sense of the word, lived a life free of reservations. Such unfussy standards are what has led him here today, to The Grande Hotel, with a mood untainted by the inclement weather.

One look at the place tells him that The Grande was the picture of opulence in its day. Now, however, it appears worn and forgotten, a crumbling love letter to grander times he remembers fondly. Even from his vantage point, with the passing of the busy traffic spraying dirty rain against the foot of the door behind him, he can see the veils of dreamcatcher cobwebs and the fine sheen of gray dust on the balustrades before they curve up and around into the gloom upstairs. Next to the stairs, a tarnished brass elevator, the floor lights blinking a slow amber pulse as whoever's entombed inside ascends with mechanical leisure. To the right of the stairs, the long mahogany reception desk, so feebly illuminated by the cracked yellow sconces on the wall, the receptionist seems a slightly crooked charcoal stroke on a faded canvas. At Desmond's approach, he straightens, only just, and fixes him with a weary gaze. In his hand, a silver pen poised over an absurdly large registration book. The lined pages are devoid of all but a handful of names.

'Good day, sir.'

Desmond nods and smiles. 'And to you. Any chance there's a vacancy?'

With all the urgency of a sloth in a funeral suit, the receptionist looks down at the book as if in its mostly blank pages he might find the answer to Desmond's question. After a prolonged moment measured only by the muted sizzle of rain and the dull tock of an unseen clock, the man raises his vulpine face and stretches it into a forced grin. His eyes are the same color as the pen, and do not seem fond of the light.

'How long will you be staying with us, sir?'

'Not very long I'd imagine. My purpose here is rather final, if you catch my drift,' he replied, trying to figure out where the man had come from - what with his thick European accent.

The receptionist studies him for a moment. His right eyebrow twitches. 'Indeed I do, sir. Our rates are fifty dollars for the night.'

'That seems entirely reasonable.' He hands over a damp fifty, which the receptionist stows in his pocket. *If his intent is to keep the money for himself,* Desmond thinks, *Good for him. Victory for the little guy. And it's not like anybody is going to know the difference.*

'Very good, sir. Please sign here.'

He turns the enormous book around to face Desmond and hands him the silver pen.

'Should I sign anywhere in particular?' Desmond asks.

'Wherever you like.'

He does.

'The dining room is unavailable, I'm afraid. We can offer room service but if that isn't enough for you, you'll see from the information packet in your room, there are a number of local eateries who would be happy to accommodate you.'

'That's fine. I don't plan to eat very much anyway.' He pats his round belly with a wizened hand. 'I'm given to dyspepsia, and other less pleasant things, but I suppose that's the price of having lived this long.'

The thin man grimaces in faux sympathy. 'I'm sorry to hear that, sir.' He moves away from the counter and plucks a single silver key from one of the hooks in a row on the wall behind him. Attached to the key is a cream, diamond shaped fob with the number 27 printed on it in suitably baroque font.

'I noticed you had a limp,' he says as he hands Desmond the key, 'So I put you on the first floor and the first door to your left as you go up the stairs.'

'Well, that's very considerate of you,' Desmond beams.

'Will you require assistance with your luggage?'

Desmond waves away the question. 'Not at all. As you can see I've only the one suitcase, and it's rather light. Wouldn't even have bothered to bring it but people would have considered it peculiar had I walked among them with ropes and knives and guns and razors cradled in my arms like some kind of mad person, don't you think?'

A single courteous nod from the receptionist. 'Indeed, sir. Will there be anything else?'

'No, I think that should do it.' Desmond places a five-dollar note on the counter. The other man looks at it as if it might be the wrapping paper from a greasy burger.

'Hardly necessary, sir.'

'I insist. You've been most kind.'

The receptionist bows and palms the money. Desmond tips his hat, turns, and makes his way up the stairs, eschewing the elevator because for one, it's still occupied, and for another, he's claustrophobic.

The carpet on the stairs is the colour of old blood, and to Desmond, this seems highly appropriate, though his appreciation of the hue is marred by the ache in his knees. Too many winters have made warped doors of his bones, his joints like un-oiled hinges. It is not a complaint, for he is not given to such pointless endeavours, but a simple fact. He is old and his time is almost at hand.

A little out of breath, his heart pounding dully against his ribs, he mounts the last quartet of steps to the first floor landing. Up here, the light is no better, the sconces veiled in cobwebs to the point of suffusion. As a result, the hallway is a chaos of shadows, the doors on either side winnowing away from him to be swallowed by the dark. He makes his way to the door of Number 27 and is surprised when the key slides smoothly into the lock and the latch turns with equal ease. Such efficiency seems contradictory in a place as gone to seed as The Grande.

The door opens without protest on a room with faded charm. It is small, but he has no need of space or extravagance, for he doesn't intend to be here long. There is a bed with a brass frame, a sturdy mattress, and a floral-patterned duvet that looks older than Desmond. The carpet is some indefinable shade of green and worn down almost to nothing. To his left, a cubby holds a toilet and a small shower. The towels appear clean. There is no TV, just a small scarred table and a rickety-looking chair. The curtains are thick, heavy, and look as if they've been fashioned from dust. The room reeks of old memories trapped in an airless space. He wondered whether all rooms were like this and - if they were - how the place was still open.

Desmond sets his suitcase on the bed and undoes the clasps. Inside are the tools of his trade: gloves (though he imagines these won't be necessary), a rope, a hunting knife, a Ruger, a scalpel, a straight razor, a hammer, and a small bottle of rat poison. He smiles and runs a gentle hand over the weapons. They have served him well for many, many years. So much so that he has more of a bond with them than he has most people. Together, they have been through a lot. They are his friends. Tonight, all going according to plan, they will assist him in one final celebration of death.

He closes the suitcase, leaving the clasps undone, and lies down on the bed next to it.

From bones to brain, he is tired. It has been a long, eventful, and satisfying adventure that has brought him to this point, but all good things must eventually end, and he can't deny that he is excited by the prospect of sleep. He has certainly earned it. The only mystery that remains now is the final one, the biggest one: what comes next? It is a question he has pondered every time he has taken a life, one that has nagged him for decades. What awaits the soul once the lights have been turned out? Heaven, hell, some other cosmic continuance of the soul's journey, or nothing at all? Perhaps the most appealing theory he has heard in his lifetime has been the one in which the soul, once freed, becomes a passenger on a train that travels through the best memories of one's earthly existence. And though Desmond does not have much faith that mere mortals can predict what follows mortality, he finds himself hoping this one is true. If it is, the afterlife will be virtually indistinguishable from the mortal one, for Desmond's life is a collection of wonderful memories. And if the next realm automatically excises the bad stuff, then it will be a virtual nirvana, for he is under no illusions that the path he has carved for himself must have in some way been instigated and influenced by the maltreatment at the hands of his drunkard parents and the foster family to which he was entrusted after their deaths. Yes, without the antagonists, the next plane will surely be a blissful one.

He looks up at the ceiling and the elaborate chandelier through which a large spider weaves an equally elaborate web, and he thinks of the couple he has come here to kill. He does not know them very well, nor does he have much of a motive for ending them. They simply chose the seat opposite him on the train. Wrong place, wrong time. This will surely complicate further the puzzle detectives and the media have been trying to solve for decades now. Murder is supposed to have a reason. From crimes of passion to revenge and everything in between, it is easier for the lateral-minded to conjure solutions when the villain's motivations are clear. However, when it's little more than compulsion driven by madness (and Desmond is under no illusions that he is sane) and, perhaps, childhood abuse, the pattern becomes harder to predict and intercept, which is why Desmond has been allowed to continue his work unimpeded for so long. There have been close calls, of course, but he is just a friendly old man, unassuming to the point of invisibility, and this is a distinct advantage for men in his chosen field. The receptionist's ambivalence to what amounts to a confession of deadly intent is just the latest example of this. The world doesn't care unless you force them to. Kill a child or a rich young debutante and the world loses its mind. Kill a poor person, and nobody bats an eye. Tell people you intend to do harm and they don't know how to process it, so they don't. Apathy is safer than caring.

Desmond laces his fingers over his chest, watches the progress of the spider. There are brown egg sacs in the web. They look full to bursting.

There were only four names in the registration book. Briefly he flirts with the idea of dispatching all of them, but that's too ambitious for a man of his age. He is already exhausted, and the man of the couple looks like he may put up a fight. Shame, really, as it would have been quite an impressive final chapter in the story of his life. He can imagine the headlines: MASSACRE AT THE GRANDE HOTEL. There would be a grainy picture of the hotel exterior in all its faltering glory, and maybe a picture of Desmond himself, smiling as always. They might even christen him with a catchy, media-friendly moniker: The Happy Killer, or The Smiling Man. The latter has an urban legend feel to it which he particularly likes.

But no, he decides it will be enough to kill the couple and then himself. He is so very tired and eager to be done with it all, because as much as he relishes the work, it is no longer as easy—and, if he's honest with himself,

as enjoyable—as it used to be.
     So, tonight the story ends.
     He smiles and closes his eyes.
     But first, sleep of a temporary kind.

Tommy and Grace

by

Shane McKenzie

'How much of that stuff did you give him?' Tommy said. 'Think maybe you gave him too much.'

'Does it really matter?' Grace glanced at the rearview mirror.

Tommy had been watching their stepfather rolling around in the back of the pickup for hours. The man's limp body slid across the truck bed every time they made a turn, the back of his head thumping across the metal grooves. The way his body kept bouncing, it was hard to tell if he was breathing or not.

'I thought you said you wanted to look him in the eyes before you...you know... Kill him,' Tommy said. 'You said, after everything he did, you wanted to—'

'I know what I said.' Grace's hands twisted around the steering wheel like she was trying to wring water out of it. 'Doesn't matter anymore.'

'I think he's dead.'

'Then he's dead. Fuck him.'

Tommy barely heard her. His eyes still on the truck bed, he realized there were supposed to be two shovels rolling around in the back with Jim's body. And he realized he was the one responsible for getting them back there.

Grace slapped the back of his head and made his forehead thunk against the small rear window. He rubbed the sore spot as he turned around in his seat. He'd been watching Jim for so long, the glaring sun blasting its rays through the windshield set his eyes on fire.

'Quit staring at him. Creeping me out.'

'Just making sure he don't wake up.'

'Thought you said he was dead.' The road curved hard to the right, and there was another heavy thump in the back.

'Looks dead. But what if he's not?' Tommy hadn't wanted any part of Grace's plan. Wanted to stay in the hospital with Mama. He thought if he talked to her long enough, maybe she'd wake up. No matter what the doctors said.

Grace reached under her seat and pulled out a black pistol, shook it like a pepper shaker. 'That's what this is for.'

Tommy wasn't sure how long they'd been driving, but it felt like they'd be reaching China any second. His stomach growled, and despite the brightness of the day, his eyelids kept trying to pinch shut. His chest still hurt when he breathed, but he didn't want to complain about it. Grace and Mama had it a lot worse than him—miles worse.

Even though he had covered his eyes the best he could, he still caught glimpses of Grace and Mama. Still saw bits and pieces of what Jim was doing to them.

I catch your eyes shut one more time, boy, and I'll make you come over here and finish the job! You'd like that, wouldn't you, boy? I said open your fuckin' eyes!

'So why don't we just pull over right here and bury him then?' Tommy said, staring out his window at the vast desert and cliffsides all around them. When he realized how high up they were, he had to look away to keep the panic down.

'Not till I know we got the right spot. Something nobody will find.'

There's nothing out here! I'm hungry and tired and I wanna go home. Mama might've already woken up by now, and she's probably worried and—'

'There!' Grace clipped the tip of Tommy's nose when she pointed.

'There what?'

'Right there, stupid. The cliffside caves in, see? We can bury him there and nobody driving by will be able to see us.'

'I don't see it.'

'Exactly. Just trust me, okay? We can—'

Tommy saw a flash of white fur half a second before they hit it. The impact threw the truck into the air and made Jim's body slam hard into the side of the metal bed.

The truck swerved while Grace fought the steering wheel, then finally got it pulled over. 'What the fuck...'

'We hit something.'

'No shit.'

They hopped out of the truck and stared silently at the flat tire for a few minutes.

'What now?' Tommy said, clutching at his aching ribs. 'Grace?'

'I'm fucking thinking!'

'How about this for what now?'

Then a fist like a knuckled cinder block slammed into the side of Grace's face. Her head bounced off the passenger window before she dropped to the concrete. Tommy tried to run, but Jim grabbed him by the back of the neck and squeezed until he thought his head would pop right off his shoulders.

Jim spat a wad of bloody mucus into the dirt, his face bruised up and bloody from the rough ride. His eyes were as red as junebugs. He tried to smile that nasty smile of his, but he couldn't hold the shape of it. Instead, he groaned and grabbed his head, looked ready to fall over, but caught himself on the side of the pickup.

'Big plans, you and your sister, huh, boy?' He shoved Tommy toward the back of the truck. Kept mumbling and cussing, but Tommy blocked him out and focused on the bloody heap lying in the road a few yards back.

Looked like an opossum, its tongue hanging from its mouth. Its white fur was stained red, more blood smeared across the street, but it was still in one piece. Looked in better shape than Grace was lying in the road behind him.

Tommy didn't realize he was crying until Jim slapped the back of his head and told him to quit it. 'Little fuckers thought you could get rid of me? Shee-it.'

'We...w-we didn't mean to—'

The next thing Tommy knew, he was taking a bite out of the tailgate. His front teeth nearly bit completely through his upper lip. With his eyes full of tears and his mouth swelling up and leaking all over the place, he let himself fall to the ground.

'You're gonna be a man before this shit's over. You hear me, boy?'

Tommy cupped his face and sobbed. When his eyes landed back on that dead opossum, he got to thinking about his mama and how he might never see her again. Thinking that this was the stupidest plan Grace had ever come up with, whether Jim deserved it or not.

All Tommy could hope for was that someone would drive by and save them, but he hadn't seen another car in the past couple hours at least. Probably why the opossum hadn't thought twice about walking across that road—probably had done it a thousand times before.

Jim disappeared for a moment, then stumbled back over with Grace draped across his shoulder. She was still out of it, but was starting to whimper a little. But when Jim slammed her down onto the tailgate, making the whole truck bounce, she woke up and got to screaming and kicking. Jim shut her back up with another knuckle sandwich.

'Stand up,' Jim said, then nudged Tommy onto his back with the tip of his boot. He pointed the pistol and cocked the hammer. 'Hear me talking, boy?'

Tommy did as he was told, his eyes bouncing from the gun's barrel to Jim's red, sweaty face. 'You gonna kill us?'

Jim laughed at that, then grabbed his head again. He was trying to act tougher than he felt, Tommy could tell. 'I'm gonna do something I should've done a long way back.' He used the gun to point at the front of Tommy's jeans. 'Pull them pants down. Underwear too.'

Tommy didn't move. Could only stare at his sister as she started to cry. Fat tears rolled out and swam sideways down her face, puddling up on the metal of the tailgate.

Jim stormed over and shoved the gun's barrel into Tommy's jean's zipper. 'You either do what I say, or I turn that little pecker of yours into a pussy and I fuck both you and your sister. That what you want, faggot? Or do you wanna follow my fucking directions?'

Tommy glanced down the road again, but they were alone. Nobody was coming. And then his jeans and underwear were bunched up at his knees and the hot air wrapped around his bare groin and butt cheeks like a heated blanket.

When Jim grabbed Grace, she screamed and tried to crawl away. Kicking her legs and scraping her nails across the truck bed. But there was nowhere to go, and Jim grabbed her by her back pockets and yanked her toward him.

After he ripped her shirt open and lifted her bra, he squeezed both of her breasts and mashed them together with the gun still in his hand, chuckling while he did it. His eyes still on her chest, he called out to

Tommy. 'Come over here and take a look. Kinda small for my taste, but not bad. Go ahead, boy. Get you a feel. Don't act like you don't want to.'

Tommy couldn't move, kept his eyes down on his hands that were cupped over his groin. He knew what Jim was going to make him do. And Tommy decided he'd rather take a bullet than do anything like that to his own sister.

Jim was too busy pulling Grace's jeans and panties down to pay any attention to Tommy. He stuffed the pistol behind his belt to free up his hands, then used them to squeeze Grace's ass the same way he had her breasts. When he spread them apart, Tommy caught a quick glimpse of pink between them, and he quickly forced himself to look away.

Jim pressed his face up against Grace's backside, taking a long sniff like it was a fresh blueberry pie. Tommy turned his head, then gasped at what he saw.

The opossum was alive. Lying on its side, struggling to get to its feet. The poor thing was hurt bad and probably wouldn't make it through the night, but it still had some life in it. When it saw Tommy watching, it froze up, went back to playing dead, but its black eyes stayed on Tommy.

Then Jim's strong grip wrapped around the back of Tommy's neck and forced him to turn back toward his sister.

Jim shoved him forward, then gave him a light pat on his bare butt. 'She's waiting. Let's see what you got, boy.'

Tommy didn't move. All he could hear was Grace crying and sniffling. She was saying something, but Tommy couldn't make out any of the words.

When the gun was pressed to the back of his head, Tommy tensed up, but still refused to move. Refused to look anywhere but at his feet.

'Shit, boy,' Jim said, then chuckled as he walked back toward Grace. 'You don't even know what to do with it, do you? Guess one more lesson won't hurt none.'

'Don't do that,' Tommy said through his teeth, but that only made Jim laugh again.

Jim unbuckled his belt, the bulge in his jeans already growing. 'Pay attention now. Cuz there's gonna be a quiz.'

The opossum was moving again, limbs flailing. It started making a choking sound, blood spraying past its teeth and painting the pavement.

Jim clamped the gun in his teeth as he pulled his pants down. Tommy watched, his eyes darting from the opossum back to Jim. He waited for the right moment, just when Jim's head dipped low enough.

'Grace!' he called, and forced himself to look at her.

She locked eyes with him, her face glistening with tears, and then she saw Jim behind her. She didn't hesitate. Her foot sprang backward, a strong horse-kick that landed dead-center in Jim's face. Squashed his nose like a cockroach. Blood blossomed on his face at the same time the gun slipped from his mouth and clattered to the road.

'Fucking cunt!'

Tommy wanted to go for the gun, but it hadn't fallen far enough away from Jim, and he was already reaching for it when Grace leapt onto his back. Her fists pounded his head and face, then she bit into his ear.

Jim screamed and spun, reaching backwards for Grace. Then he gave up on her and started back for the gun, but by then, Tommy was already running toward his own weapon.

This time, when the opossum saw him coming, it didn't bother with playing dead. It kicked its feet faster, desperate to roll onto them and either run or defend itself. Its bloodstained teeth snapped between growls and hisses.

Tommy ran around it, almost getting his ankle bit, and wrapped his fingers around the critter's ropey tail. When he lifted the thing upside down off the pavement, it started screeching and wiggling its body, clawing and snapping at Tommy.

Making sure he kept it at arm's length, Tommy sprinted back toward the truck. And not a second too early.

Jim had shrugged Grace off his back, making her fly off and slam the back of her head against the tailgate before crumbling up on the ground. He had the gun in his hand. Wiped the blood from his ear and looked at it in his palm, then pointed the gun at Grace.

'Hey, asshole!' Tommy said, and flung the opossum underhand like a softball pitch.

Jim turned and didn't even have time to look surprised. The opossum hit him in the chest, and it wasn't until it was on Jim that Tommy realized how big the thing was.

Its mouth slammed shut over Jim's face, teeth digging into his busted nose and the bottom of his chin. As Jim screamed and dropped to the concrete, the opossum got to kicking its legs, slicing Jim's throat and chest. As long as it was, the thing's hind legs reached all the way down to Jim's groin, which was still out in the open. It only took a few seconds before everything down there looked like a mess of bloody meat, strips of skin and god knows what hanging down as the claws shredded it all to hell.

No matter how hard he pulled, Jim couldn't get the opossum off. He screamed and tried to shoot the thing off him, but only managed to fire bullets into the desert air, the sky purple and pink as the sun dipped away.

He rolled away from the truck, and Tommy ran straight for Grace, pulling his pants up as he went. She was throwing her shirt back on when he got to her, and when she saw it was him, she threw her arms around him and pulled him close.

Jim growled, grabbing two fistfuls of furry flesh and yanking as hard as he could manage. And he finally pulled the critter loose. His face bright red and striped with open wounds, he had a moment to smile in triumph before he went over the side of the cliff. Opossum and all. Neither one of them making a sound on their way down.

Tommy and Grace sprinted to the edge of the road and peered down. Tommy thought he could make out the shape of a crooked body, but it could have been anything.

'Told you this spot was perfect,' Grace said, then massaged her jaw where a bruise was already darkening her skin.

'I feel kinda bad,' Tommy said, staring down into the dark nothing.

'And why the fuck would you say something like that, Tommy?'

Tommy shrugged. 'Opossum didn't deserve that.'

Grace punched him in the shoulder and laughed, then wrapped her arm around his neck and pulled him away from the cliff back toward the truck.

'What now?' Tommy said as they both sat on the tailgate.

'Haven't thought that far ahead.'

He nodded. 'I forgot the shovels.'

'What?'

'The shovels. You told me to grab them and I forgot. Scared to tell you till now.'

She laughed again, then kissed the side of his head. 'You're such a dork.'

Tommy wasn't sure how long they'd sat there like that, staring at the stars and trying to find patterns in them. He almost forgot why they had come out there in the first place and everything that happened after. But when the headlights hit them, it all came flooding back, and he wished he had the gun or the shovels, or even another opossum.

But the station wagon slowed down, then stopped beside them. The passenger window rolled down and the driver leaned over and smiled. The guy looked harmless enough, reminded Tommy of his math teacher back home.

'Car trouble?' the man said as he turned down his talk radio.

'Something like that,' Grace said. 'Hit and run. Banged us up pretty bad, then the bastard just took off. Truck ain't going nowhere.'

When the man glanced at Tommy, all Tommy could think to do was nod.

'Nasty business. I don't usually pick up strangers from the side of the road, but I wouldn't be able to sleep if I left you kids out here alone like this.' He smiled like he was trying to be playful. 'You aren't dangerous, are you?'

'Wouldn't hurt a fly,' Grace said.

'Or an opossum,' Tommy added.

The man thought about that for a moment, but then shrugged, reached over, and unlocked the passenger door. 'You're in luck. There's a hotel only a few more miles up the road. Why don't you let me get a room for you and get some food in your belly? Then in the morning, we can report this little boom and zoom here, hm?'

Tommy and Grace shared a quick look, and for a second, Tommy thought his sister was going to tell the guy to fuck off. After everything they had been through, he wouldn't have blamed her for not trusting him. But he sure was glad when she climbed into the station wagon and waved him in.

'Warm beds and full tummies coming right up,' the man said, then turned his talk radio back up and drove down the road.

Craig O'Dell
by
David Moody

'You must be relieved it's over?'

'Odd choice of word. It's a great weight lifted, though I'm not sure if relieved is perhaps quite right. On a personal level, I can't deny that my exoneration has relieved me of an unbearable weight, but any positive emotions I might be feeling are tempered by feelings of deep, deep sorrow for the boy. A young life needlessly and tragically cut short.'

'Quite.'

'William was a troubled soul. I knew that from the moment I first met him.'

'When was that again?'

'Last April. I'd not long moved to the parish. I really thought I'd be able to help.'

'Wait . . . do you mind if I take a few notes?'

'What?'

'I'm sorry to interrupt. Look, I know the verdict has only just been announced, but the sooner we get the press release drafted and approved, the sooner you can move on and put this behind you.'

'Of course. Though we all have lessons to be learnt as a result of what happened to William. It's certainly not all over because the coroner and judge say so. There is a higher authority to consider here.'

'Without doubt. Look, Reverend, I've dealt with a couple of similar high-profile cases over the last few months. Other priests have told me they can find this part of the process quite cathartic.'

'A replacement confessional? We're not Catholic, Iain.'

'Heaven forbid!'

'I'll pretend I didn't hear that.'

'I'm sorry if I sound flippant, I don't mean to be disrespectful. It's just that I believe these sessions can feel like a very basic form of therapy. Again, I'm sorry if that sounds a little grand or even offensive, it's just . . .'

'Just what?'

'Just that I often wonder if someone in your position is ever really able to fully talk about how they're feeling? You spend all your time listening to other people and helping them, but who listens to you?'

'You're relatively new to the church, aren't you, Iain.'

'Is it that obvious?'

'I'm afraid it is, but that's no bad thing. I believe we benefit from new blood and fresh ideas. There's a danger we might otherwise become stuck in our ways, something I fear the church has been guilty of in the past. Tell me, what's your background.'

'The corporate machine, I'm afraid. I've always worked in press and PR, but in construction and media, mostly.'

'And what prompted the change?'

'I wanted to do something more worthwhile, something where people mattered more than profits and outputs.'

'Then I'm glad you've found your calling. We're blessed to have you. In answer to your question, Iain, my faith supports me and it is all I need. As long as I'm doing right in the eyes of God, then I have no need for anything else. He gives me all the support and encouragement I need, and He guides me to make the right decisions for the right reasons. You must understand, entering the priesthood isn't a decision anyone takes lightly. One has to be aware of the implications from the outset. I'd be less than honest if I said I hadn't had moments of real personal doubt – several recently, in fact – but my faith helps me through even the toughest of challenges. Any difficulties I might have faced are trivial when you compare them to the life of Christ, don't you agree?'

'Oh yes, of course. Again, I hope I'm not talking out of turn . . .'

'Not at all. It's important to be open and honest, isn't it? Talking like this can only help.'

'Absolutely. Good. Thank you. So, if you don't mind, can you tell me a little about your time in Waltherstow parish? Obviously I know about your background and the timescales, but I'd like to hear something of your take on events, if that's okay? It'll help inform the press release and any follow-up enquiries we might receive.'

'Of course. As you know, when I first arrived in the parish it was clear that there was much work to be done. We priests are only human, after all. My predecessor did a wonderful job but . . .'

'But what?'

'But I guess it's inevitable that, to some degree, we look at everything through our eyes, no matter how hard we might try otherwise.'

'I don't follow.'

'Forgive me, I'm tired. It's been a long and testing day. Please do stop me if I'm not making sense.'

'Go on.'

'What I mean is, it's easy to slip into routine, isn't it? It's one of the reasons the church moves priests around. As I said, we're only human, and though we try consciously to relate to *all* of our parishioners, regardless of age and circumstance, on a subconscious level that's harder than it might seem. We each have an unconscious bias, I believe. The previous incumbent of my role, the late Reverend Wilkins, was in his early seventies when he passed away and had spent more than a decade in Waltherstow. It was hard for him to relate to the younger people in the parish and, unfortunately, that showed. I'm being careful here not to sound critical, because Reverend Wilkins did a huge amount of truly wonderful work here, and it wouldn't have been the place it is today had it not been for his efforts.'

'Yes, I've spoken to a number of people who knew him. He was quite a character, by all accounts.'

'That's what I've heard too. He was certainly well-loved in the parish. Again, though, and I don't want this to sound negative at all, but the youth connection perhaps wasn't quite as strong as it might have been.'

'He'd lost touch?'

'I think that's a little strong.'

'But this is where you came in?'

'Yes. I saw it as my mission to reach out to those the church had left behind. I introduced all-age worship, re-started junior church, and set up a youth club at the community centre.'

'And that was where you first met William.'

'That's right. The community hall was in a miserable, dilapidated state when I arrived, so I instigated a project to do something about it. I visited the local schools and colleges to drum up support. I sold it to the kids by telling them it was their centre, so it was up to them what it became. I was giving them a chance to make their mark and shape things. I let them do anything they wanted . . . within reason, of course.'

'Of course. And you had a good response?'

'A very positive response, yes. I didn't expect hundreds to turn out, but there were enough volunteers to be able to give the building a facelift, inside and out. And by doing that, I thought the kids would become emotionally invested in the place. To relate things back to your previous vocation, Iain, I wanted them to feel less like customers and more like shareholders. Does that make sense?'

'Absolutely.'

'William didn't arrive until the second or third weekend, as I recall. I could immediately tell that he was a deeply troubled lad, and I made a particular effort to make sure he was fully involved in the project. I think I tried a little too hard.'

'What do you mean?'

'A moment ago I mentioned how I believed Reverend Wilkins appealed more to the older people in the parish because he was older himself. They naturally gravitated towards each other. I think . . . and this is difficult to explain . . . that William took something of a shine to me. He was young and confused . . . vulnerable. I was the first person to have taken any interest in him in a long time, and I think he struggled to know how to deal with that. It's difficult to expect a lonely and isolated thirteen year old boy like William to understand the relationship between a priest and his parishioners or, indeed, between a priest and God.'

'He ignored the boundaries?'

'It's not so much he ignored the boundaries, more that he just wasn't aware of them.'

'Tell me more . . .'

'If I'm honest, I think I was naïve, and I bitterly regret my actions now. Everything I did was done with the very best of intentions, but in retrospect it backfired horribly. I was trying to encourage William to come out of his shell and be more positive about himself and his own self-image, and he misconstrued my attentions. He thought I was offering him more than I was.'

'I can see you're upset, Reverend. Do you want to stop? We can finish this later . . .?'

'No, no. I'd rather get this over and done with.'

'As long as you're sure?'

'I am. You know, I think you may be right – perhaps this is a form of therapy after all. I just wish I'd been able to help William. I'm afraid I pushed him away.'

'How? That's not how the hearing viewed it.'

'I think the poor lad had taken a real shine to me, and I mistook that for enthusiasm for the community centre project and the church as a whole. I was blind to his affections. Unbeknownst to me he'd developed something of an infatuation, and all the time I thought I was helping, I was actually just perpetuating the illusion. Fanning the flames, if you like.'

'He made several approaches to you, didn't he?'

'He did. It was a failure on my part not to fully appreciate his intent. The judge pointed that out in no uncertain terms. Everything I did was done with the absolute best of intentions, but I allowed myself to be placed in a compromising position and I didn't realise until it was too late. When I reacted and tried to set the record straight with him . . .'

'. . . he reacted too.'

'Precisely.'

'And that was where the accusations of abuse stemmed from.'

'That's right. You know, I ask forgiveness every single day because I made such a basic mistake allowing William into my home and it had such dire ramifications. There were no witnesses to what happened in the house. If I'd just had someone else there, or if I'd been more measured in my enthusiasm to involve him in the church, then maybe all of this could have been avoided and a young life might have been saved.'

'Reverend, I sat through the entire hearing and heard all the evidence and all the statements. I think you're being exceptionally hard on yourself. Off the record, as I see it, I think your only crime was caring too much.'

'God bless you, Iain.'

'I can only begin to imagine how this must have affected you, particularly when the boy took his life.'

'It's been the most testing of times. Physically, emotionally, spiritually . . . a situation like this makes you question everything. It tests your faith.'

'I'm sure it does.'

'You know, we live in an increasingly fractured and secular world. It's become all too easy and fashionable to blame God or blame the church. You open a newspaper or turn on the TV and watch the news, and every day you hear about the sins of priests and reports of large scale abuse. The good the church does is so often overlooked. I don't blame William for what he said about me. He was hurting.'

'He alleged that you abused him on a number of occasions.'

'He did. But, as you heard, he could provide no evidence and the experts who tried to help him recognised that no abuse had taken place and that he'd fabricated his entire story. He made the whole thing up because he believed that I'd rejected him, that I'd turned my back on him like everyone else had. He thought I had something more than a spiritual concern for him. He saw the media headlines and decided to write some of his own.'

'And then . . .'

'I just wish I could have stopped him, Iain. When his lies were exposed there was no one there to catch him as he fell and he took his own life.'

'It was desperately sad.'

'And avoidable. I still feel I should have done more, and I ask God for guidance and forgiveness every day.'

'Again off the record, Reverend, I don't believe there was anything more you could have done. That boy was broken long before you found him.'

*

Father Craig O'Dell left the building through a discreet side entrance and headed straight for the car park. He was drained. Emotionally shattered. Empty. In need of a drink.

He drove back through the grim evening rush hour. The pissing rain slowed everything to a crawl, and the lack of speed made his guts churn. Were they all looking at him? He kept his collar turned up and his head down. He didn't want anyone to recognise him. So things had worked out in his favour today, but it was all over the papers and as an online confidant had told him recently, *shit sticks*. On this occasion he genuinely hadn't done anything. He hadn't touched the kid, hadn't behaved inappropriately, hadn't said anything he shouldn't have. He hadn't even liked him very much. Whiney little prick.

William Brent, that miserable little self-pitying cunt, had stitched him up good and proper.

*

Back to the vicarage. Christ, he needed to get away from this place. The answerphone was full of messages (from other needy fuckers, inevitably) and the doormat was covered in post. He didn't bother with any of it. Emails were a different matter, of course. He didn't have time to check them now, he just did what he had to do. He removed the hard drive and threw it in his bag.

Dog collar gone. Suitcase packed.

Reverend O'Dell left the vicarage just before eight and arrived at the hotel a little after ten. It had taken him a while to find somewhere to stay, but this place was perfect. No one knew him here. No one was interested, either.

He sat on the end of his king-size bed with a drink in his hands and weighed up his options.

If he was honest, he was surprised he'd got away with it for this long. He'd never expected the William business to be concluded in his favour. It had been a wake-up call. A not-so-gentle reminder of the risks he'd been taking.

He had a couple of associates who'd sailed this close to the wind who had given him advice. He'd struck up a wonderful online friendship with a chap called Patrick (also a man of the cloth) who'd had a similar experience and had ended up in Darfur of all places, still plying his trade with the little ones, but free as a bird. Craig had always fancied visiting Africa, but Thailand seemed a better option for now. Phuket. He'd always liked the sound of that place. *If you fancy it, Phuket*, another online friend used to call it.

He finished his drink and poured himself another.

He'd had a good run. It had lasted longer than he expected, but all good things must come to an end. *There's no smoke without fire*, Patrick in Darfur had said when Craig messaged him with the judge's verdict. *They'll be looking closer at you now. Get out while the going's good and look elsewhere.*

Sound advice.

Father Craig O'Dell had never laid a finger on William, never even wanted to (he wasn't his type – at least five years too old), but he'd fucked and fingered plenty of others before him.

<u>Carl</u>
by
Jeff Strand

'Dad! Hurry up!'

Carl sighed. He hadn't even made it two paragraphs into the article on Jennifer Lawrence in the latest issue of *Entertainment Weekly*. He'd known that the chances of him reading an entire article were non-existent, but he'd hoped to make it through at least one column.

'In a minute!' he called out.

'Daaaaaad! Hurry! I have to gooooo!'

'So do I!'

'I'm gonna pee my pants!' Ronnie began to pound on the bathroom door. 'I have to pee! I have to pee! I have to peeee!'

Carl set the magazine on the edge of the bathtub. He hadn't even started his bowel movement yet. He stood up, pulled up his pants, and opened the door in defeat. His five-year-old son sprinted past him.

After the sounds of tinkling stopped, Ronnie walked out of the bathroom. 'You forgot to flush,' said Carl.

'Huh?'

'You didn't flush the toilet.'

'When?'

'Just now!'

'Oh.'

'So do it.'

'Okay.' Ronnie returned to the bathroom.

'I don't hear it flushing,' said Carl, a moment later.

'I had to pee again.'

Finally, the toilet flushed and Ronnie emerged. 'Thank you,' said Carl.

'Can I have a strawberry Pop-Tart?'

'No.'

Carl tuned out the screaming fit. He walked back toward the doorway to relief, but just before he was able to step inside, his sixteen-year-old daughter Vanessa came out of her bedroom.

'You're not going in there, are you?' she asked.

'That was my plan, yeah,' said Carl.

'Were you going to be quick? I need to get ready.'

'Can you give me ten minutes?'

'Ten minutes?' asked Vanessa. 'What are you going to do in there, have a baby?'

'Don't be gross.'

'Can't you wait if you're doing a number two? I'm going out with Stacie and Jenny.'

'Isn't it a school night?' Carl asked.

'I'll be home by curfew. We're just going to see a movie.'

'If you're only seeing a movie, why do you need to hog the bathroom?'

'I still have to look good. I don't know who we'll run into.'

'You'll be in the dark.'

Vanessa rolled her eyes. 'Not on the way in and out of the theater. All I want to do is take a shower without it stinking in there! Jeez!'

'All right, all right,' said Carl. 'The bathroom's yours.'

Five people in a house with one bathroom was not the most convenient living arrangement. But the home was affordable, close to a good school, and the neighbors were quiet. The sacrifice had seemed worth it. In fact, it hadn't even seemed like it would be a sacrifice. Bathroom time was no big deal, right?

*

'It's all I want,' Carl told Warren, who worked in the cubicle next to his. 'To be able to sit down, enjoy a magazine article all the way through, and poop in a leisurely fashion. I never realized how much I could want this. I have fantasies about it. I used to have fantasies about my wife turning bisexual, but those are gone. What's happened to me? I used to have *real* aspirations.'

'Why not take a dump here at work?' asked Warren. 'There are three stalls. Nobody's going to knock on the door and tell you to hurry up. It's not like you take cigarette breaks.'

Carl shook his head. 'Nah. I just can't.'

If somebody came into the stall next to him, he'd freeze up and just sit there, desperately waiting for them to leave. On one nightmarish afternoon, he'd been in the middle stall, partially through the excretion process, when two men came in and took the stalls on each side of him. They were in no hurry to finish. Carl had sat there, sweating, praying that they'd just drop their respective deuces and go. Then he wondered if they were trying to wait *him* out. Did they know it was him in there? Did they think he was constipated? Were they taking glee in his misery?

'Just can't what?' asked Heather from Remittance Processing, walking into their aisle.

'He can't pinch a loaf at work,' Warren informed her.

'Ew.'

'Don't ew. I said he *can't* pinch a loaf. I didn't say that he goes around pinching loaves on random desks.'

'People should save that for their own homes,' said Heather. 'It's not a productive use of company time, and it creates a less pleasant bathroom environment for those of us who just have to pee.'

'His issue is that there are too many interruptions at home,' said Warren. 'That's why I was suggesting that he make use of the facilities in this building.'

'Let's not talk about this anymore,' said Carl.

'You're the one who started the conversation,' said Warren.

'With you! In a whisper!'

Warren was the only person Carl could talk to about embarrassing issues like this. Not that they'd been friends for a long time (they'd only worked together for two years) or were particularly close (they never socialized outside of the office). It was just that Warren had no filter. During Carl's first day at the new job, he learned that Warren shaved his pubic hair, had a false alarm herpes scare the prior month, had a thing for women who were thirty-five to fifty pounds overweight, liked to swallow gum, thought pedophiles of both genders should have their genitalia sizzled away by hydrochloric acid, preferred baths to showers, often retreated to the rarely used Conference Room 6D if he needed to fart, was not entirely opposed to getting slapped in the face during sex, ate asparagus three times a week, had once waxed his chest and would never do so again, and thought Phoebe was still the hottest of the *Friends*.

Carl had not embraced his candor.

But the onslaught of too much information continued, and eventually Carl became okay with the idea of sharing some intimate details. He'd said that, yes, even though they'd been married for eighteen years and had three kids, he and Vivian still did it doggy-style on occasion. He'd admitted that his first prostate exam had been a source of anxiety for several months beforehand, but it turned out to not be that big of a deal; unpleasant, yet worth it for the peace of mind it afforded. He'd almost shared that he had a small birthmark on his scrotum, but ultimately reconsidered.

'Why can't you just go home at lunchtime?' asked Heather.

'My commute is too long.'

'How long is it?'

'Twenty minutes.'

'So, twenty minutes there, twenty minutes back...that gives you five minutes. Do you need more than that?'

'You don't understand his point at all,' said Warren. 'He doesn't want to take a hasty dump. His whole dilemma is that he wants to be able to relax, take his time, enjoy the experience. Rushing home for a five-minute squat defeats the whole purpose.'

'My mistake,' said Heather.

'Also, when would he actually have lunch? Do you want him to eat a sandwich on the toilet? That's gross.'

'I assumed he'd eat in the car.'

'You shouldn't eat while you're driving. It's dangerous. Eyes on the road at all times.'

'I was just trying to help.'

'Well, clearly you didn't have all the information you needed before you started offering insight. I hope you've learned a little lesson.'

'I have, I'll never do it again.'

'Glad to hear it.'

Heather gave Carl a polite nod. 'Good luck pooping.'

'Uh, thanks.'

Heather left. Carl knew his face was burning. He swiveled his chair back toward his computer and tried to go back to work.

'What if you built an outhouse in your backyard?' Warren asked.

'Are you kidding me?'

'What? It's not like your daughter would want to prep for a date in an outhouse. You'd have privacy.'

'I share a backyard with four other neighbors. I can't have them staring at a damn outhouse.'

'Well, obviously, you'd have to put up a fence, too.'

'I'm not going to build a fence so that I can build an outhouse so that I can stink up my backyard. We have barbecues back there! Nobody wants to eat hamburgers and hot dogs fifteen feet from an outhouse! The whole point of this was comfort! If I do that, I'd have to spend the whole time worrying about spiders crawling on my ass!'

'You should probably keep your voice down,' Warren noted.

Carl lowered his voice. 'Anyway, other people have worse problems than this. At least I have indoor plumbing. It's no big deal. I'll be okay.'

'I'm sure you will.'

'Let us never speak of this again.'

'I'm okay with that.'

'Thank you.'

'Get laid last night?'

'None of your business.'

'So that's a no?'

'That's a 'it's none of your business."

'I didn't either.'

'Sorry to hear that.'

'I did on Saturday, though,' said Warren. 'One of those dating sites. She didn't look anything like her picture, but what was I going to do, send her home? I'd already made the spaghetti.'

'An online date agreed to meet at your apartment?' Carl asked.

'Yeah. Good thing for her I wasn't a serial killer, huh? I put all of my knives away before she got there, just so she wouldn't see any of them and feel uncomfortable.'

'That was very considerate.'

'She scraped me with her teeth. You can still see the scratch mark. She got the job done, though. Credit where it's due.'

'I'm getting back to work.'

'I wasn't going to show you the scratch. That would be unprofessional.'

'I'm getting back to work.'

'I wouldn't show you the scratch even if you asked. Not even in selfie form. You'll just have to use your imagination.'

'I'm getting back to work.'

'I'll neither confirm nor deny if I left any tooth marks on her.'

'Seriously, Warren, I've got a lot of work to do. You're going to get us written up.'

'All right, all right. Have you ever considered getting a hotel room?'

'Let it go, Warren.'

*

As Carl drove home, he thought about what Warren had said.

Getting a hotel room for the express purpose of going to the bathroom in peace was completely absurd. It was one of the dumbest ideas in the history of civilization. Human beings with self-respect simply didn't *do* that sort of thing.

On the other hand...

No! There was no other hand! No way in hell was he going to pay for a hotel room just to shit. That was completely out of the question. One hundred percent. Not a chance.

Yet, didn't he deserve this? He was a good father. He was a good husband. He provided for his family. He worked hard. Sacrificed. Put the happiness of others before his own.

Would giving himself one lengthy, uninterrupted, completely private, silent (except for his own body noises), peaceful bowel movement really be such a bad thing? It would be a one-time event. Something he could look back upon with fondness. He could return to that happy memory when he was hastily trying to squeeze one out with his children pounding on the door.

He couldn't believe he was actually considering this.

He'd be doing nothing wrong. He wasn't cheating on his wife. He wasn't lying to her. He was, he supposed, spending money without telling her, but it wasn't a major purchase. Vivian bought things that cost more than a hotel room without discussing it with him first.

Why should he deprive himself of this moment of bliss?

He'd do it. He owed it to himself. It would keep him from becoming resentful, and that was good for everyone.

Obviously, he couldn't pay with a credit card, because he'd have to explain why there was a hotel room charge, but socking away a little bit of cash here and there would go unnoticed. And it would give him something to look forward to.

Carl grinned. He felt better than he had in a very long time.

*

A few weeks later, he took off work two hours early, and pulled into the parking lot of The Grande.

Honour

by

Gary McMahon

Yasmin had stopped screaming several minutes ago but her body continued to burn.

Even as his surroundings slipped in and out of focus – the light dimming, the air filling with tiny stars – Pete could still smell the sickly-sweet aroma of roasting human meat and feel the oily heat of the dying fire pressing against his exposed skin.

He tried not to look but his eyes refused to obey the command and he sat there staring at the ravaged, smoking remains of the woman he loved. He couldn't move from the chair; his hands were bound behind him with stiff rope and the same kind of rope was wrapped and knotted around his thighs, attaching them to the chair. But the bonds that kept him there were more than physical.

There was nowhere left for him to run.

All the running they had done before this moment had led them only here: to this abandoned warehouse on the outskirts of the city where his love now lay in flames.

'See what you made me do, Yaz?' Rizwan stood a few feet away from the burning remains, just out of reach of the heat and the spitting hot fat. His shaved head was bowed. His muscular arms hung loose at his sides. 'I didn't want it to be like this.' He glanced at Pete, his dark eyes watery, on the verge of tears.

'Bastard.' It was all Pete could manage. He spat out the word, like poison in his mouth. There was so much more to say, but he no longer possessed the energy to speak.

'It was all your fault. Both of you, for the shame you have brought upon our family. I didn't want to kill her.'

Pete remembered this squat, unsmiling man pouring the petrol over Yasmin's body, laughing as she squirmed in pain and panic at his feet.

Are you scared yet? That's what he'd said, excitement in his voice

'I was only trying to scare her.'

When he'd lit the match, his eyes had caught and held the glare of the naked flame and shone, making him look manic, as if some other, stranger being stared out from behind them.

'I didn't want her to…to die.'

Pete's head drooped. He closed his eyes. No matter how hard he tried, he couldn't rid himself of the image of Yasmin twisting and twitching in the fire, her clothes, hair, flesh all burning, the stench filling the room.

Rizwan went quiet. He shuffled backwards, a yard or two away from his sister's corpse. The flames were dying properly now. Fat popped and sizzled, but the heat was reducing. Rizwan grabbed a large piece of tarpaulin from the floor nearby, unfolding it as he approached the evidence of his madness. Pausing for just a second, he threw the sheet over her body and began to stamp on it, putting out the remaining flames.

'You did this to yourself. You shamed us all.' His voice was a whisper.

Behind Pete, a heavy door opened and then slammed shut. Footsteps sounded on the concrete floor, quick and light.

Rizwan looked over Pete's head, his face registering fear.

'What have you done?' Tariq walked past Pete and stood before his younger brother. 'What the fuck have you done?'

Rizwan could only shake his head.

'I told you to tie them up and wait for me.'

Rizwan tried to smile but the expression twisted his narrow face into a hideous mask.

Tariq stepped forward and grabbed his younger brother by the face, wrapping a thin, long-fingered hand around his jaw. He pushed him backwards, making the younger man shuffle and almost lose his footing.

'I'm sorry.' Rizwan's voice was garbled because he was speaking through the barrier of Tariq's hand. 'She wouldn't listen…'

Tariq was much taller, slimmer, and more agile than his brother. He brought his back foot forward, wrapping it around the other man's calf, and took him easily to the ground. As Rizwan went down, Tariq slapped him hard across the face. 'This is not what Uncle wanted!'

Rizwan cowered like a trapped animal, bringing up his hands in a defensive gesture. 'I had no choice…she…she had a knife.' He pointed to the blade, where it had landed on the floor during the struggle. 'She cut me.' He showed Tariq the small bloodstain on his sleeve, caused when the kitchen knife had slashed at his forearm, causing a tiny wound.

'You always fuck up. Uncle should have sent me to get her alone.' Tariq turned away and walked quickly towards Pete. His face was blank, expressionless. Pete opened his mouth to speak, but Tariq threw a straight punch, catching him on the side of the face. Pete's cheekbone stung; heat engulfed the area, mingling with his renewed rage.

'We'll have to kill this one now, to cover our tracks.' Then, lowering their voices, they began to converse in Punjabi – at least that's what he guessed it was, he couldn't understand a word they were saying.

Any slim promise of mercy Pete might have hoped for vanished in that instant. He realised now that both of the brothers were insane. Before he'd thought it was only Rizwan, the loose cannon, a man with no control over his emotions or the resultant actions. Now he knew that true madness manifested in different ways.

Whatever the case, he was fucked.

Even during the sudden act of violence, Tariq had not met his gaze. The man turned his back, dismissing his victim, barely even seeing him as human. 'Come with me,' he said to his younger sibling.

Rizwan got to his feet and followed his brother, head down, arms limp, posture submissive. As they passed by Pete, in his chair, Rizwan smiled at him and whispered 'Are you scared yet?'

The door opened and then clicked shut. Quieter this time. More controlled.

Pete scanned the room. They'd brought him and Yasmin here in the back of a van, trussed up like livestock, badly beaten, already weak from the chase. He'd blacked out a few times as they tied him into the wooden chair and started to question, and then slap, punch, kick, Yasmin until she curled up on the ground like a frightened child.

Tariq had left the room to call their uncle in Pakistan, or perhaps to arrange a way of getting Yasmin out of the country and back to the family home, and Rizwan's mood had changed. Become sexual. He'd started touching Yasmin, saying that she was tainted meat, no longer his sister, and he could do what he wanted.

She'd pulled the knife, slashing at him. He'd yelped, and then beaten her until she stopped struggling.

Quite why there were cans of petrol in the old warehouse, Pete would never know, but Rizwan had grabbed one and splashed its contents over his sister, laughing and taunting her.

Then, without warning, he'd lit the match and dropped it into her hair.

'Think,' said Pete. 'Think, you bastard. There must be a way out.'

There was a window opposite, but he was tied into the chair…the old, rickety wooden chair. Shifting his weight, he tried to move the chair an inch across the smooth concrete floor. The legs slid in a hitching manner across the floor. Not much, but they moved. The chair joints creaked.

The old chair. The rickety chair.

The old rickety wooden chair that might just break if he applied enough pressure…

His hands were tied behind him and they'd bound his thighs together, but his legs were free from the knees down. Struggling, he managed to just about stand in a low crouch. He eyed up the opposite wall, the window, the distance between his current position and this possible escape route.

He glanced one final time at the tarpaulin-covered mound which was all that remained of the woman he loved.

Then he started to move. In a clumsy, limping gait, he propelled himself forward as fast as he could, towards the wall. At the last minute, he swivelled his body and dropped his shoulder, as if he were trying to barge through a locked door. His momentum carried him into the wall, slamming his body against the rough breeze blocks. He felt something give in his shoulder, heard a loud cracking sound, and then he was sprawling on the floor, the chair coming apart at the joints, the ropes around his legs loosening as he writhed.

Pain lanced from his shoulder along his arm, blooming at the wrist. He had no idea how many bones he'd broken, but adrenalin kept the worst of the pain at bay for the moment. He brought his arms down and under his feet, ignoring the white-hot jolt of pain as he did so. His wrists were still bound, of course, but now he was out of the chair.

He went to the window. It was shuttered, but there was a lever to the right-hand side of the frame. Using both hands, he wound up the shutter, expecting the brothers to come through the door at any minute and catch him in the act.

His luck held.

The shutters opened.

On the other side of the window the sloped ground dropped away to a low-level car park. It wasn't a long drop, but he was already injured and he might just cause himself more damage.

'Fuck it,' he said, backing up, away from the window. 'Fuck it all.'

He ran, and hit the glass at speed, shattering it, cutting his face and neck as he went through, his waist catching the bottom rail and pitching him forward into a roll as he hit open air.

He fell awkwardly but the pain he experienced simply blended into the greater pain that now lived inside his body, a protean creature had begun to nurture. When he stopped rolling, he paused and looked back, at the broken window, and saw Yasmin standing on the other side, waving. His eyes were unable to focus properly, but he was sure it was her, urging him to keep on running, saying goodbye.

Movement was becoming difficult, but somehow he managed to get to his feet and run. He was bent over at the waist, bleeding, gasping for breath, but he kept moving forward.

Up ahead, Yasmin appeared again. She motioned for him to follow her. Turning her back, she led him away from the warehouse. Pete knew that he was hallucinating – which probably meant that his injuries were severe and the chemicals in his body were acting in self-preservation – but he embraced the illusion, using it to drive himself onwards. The woman he loved wanted him to survive. She wanted that more than anything, so much in fact that her desire had transcended death.

'I'm coming...'

She moved slowly ahead of him, keeping the distance between them regular. He knew that she wouldn't slow down, nor would she speed up. She would retain the same pace, drawing him forward, forcing him to run as best he could. She always had done, ever since he'd first met her in that pub on the high street. She'd drawn him in, kept him moving forward, convinced him that his life had meaning and he was a good man, someone who could achieve things. But only if he kept on moving forward and never looked back at the ruins of his former life: the destructive relationships, the eleven year-old son he had never met, the family members who had either died or deserted him. All the shit he had waded through just to get here...

Yasmin had always known the secret: perpetual forward motion. It was the only thing that might save him.

Across the car park: a dense stand of trees. He aimed towards it, blinking, trying to remain conscious. The pain was a throbbing thing, a beast that devoured him inch by inch, but beyond those trees, perhaps in a small clearing, he knew that his love waited for him.

Just as he walked into the trees, he heard shouting behind him.

Yasmin's brothers.

They had discovered his absence. He tried to move faster but knew that he was probably moving slower than he had done before, despite the head start. Just keep going, keep fighting. Never stop.

He lost his footing and tumbled down another steep incline, slamming his injured body against the hard ground. Gritting his teeth, he rode it out: pain was mandatory, suffering was optional. Pete chose not to suffer.

He came to rest at the bottom of the slope, sweating, pissing himself; watching with detached interest the explosions in his vision and feeling as if he had been cast adrift from the world. But through it all, he saw her, beckoning, urging him up onto his feet and deeper into the trees.

A voice not too far behind him, shouting, and full of amusement: 'Are you scared yet?'

He knew he should recognise the voice, but it was just out of reach.

Panting, limping, stumbling against tree trunks, he moved forward. The voice faded; whoever it was, they obviously couldn't see him, were just shouting into the void in the hope that he might hear and become even more fearful.

Weeks, days, hours, minutes, seconds later he emerged into a clearing. A wide field stretched before him, flat and green and bright beneath the lowering sun. In the middle of the field was stood a figure. She was now dressed in traditional Pakistani clothing. A modest outfit she'd once told him was called a *shalwar kameez*: simple trousers with a brightly coloured, subtly decorated body dress worn over the top. Jewels sparkled in the sunlight. Her face was partly covered with a neatly folded *hijab*, but he knew it was her.

It was his beloved, his little princess.

Suddenly she burst into flames, the light from her body merging with that of the dying sun. The sight did not shock him. It was natural, something that was meant to be – as much a part of normality as the sun rising and setting, the night following the day, the tides of the seas. She turned inside a cocoon of flames, dancing. Even now, she was beautiful.

As he walked slowly and painfully in her direction, the rear wall of a stark, featureless building loomed into focus behind her. It was a large place that looked like it might be a hostel or a hotel, almost certainly offering some kind of protection.

She was leading him there.

Perhaps he could find shelter in this place, someone to help him: sanctuary, at least of a temporary kind.

Are you scared yet?

It was a question someone had asked him recently. Or had it been a long time ago? He could not remember. The past had become the present had become the future: it was all one thing, flowing in a circle without end.

The blazing, shimmering figure turned and walked slowly towards the building, signalling with a flaming upraised hand for him to follow.

No, Pete wasn't scared, not any more. But deep down, he knew that he should be.

Iain

by

Jasper Bark

No one ever realises how close they are to murder, Iain mused. They think they have all the time in the world. That they can go about their humdrum, little lives as they always have and see their plans through to fruition. They have no idea what they've got coming.

Iain put down the binoculars. He was parked across the street from a grotty, little two bedroom terrace. A grey haired woman in a stained cardigan was standing on the doorstep smoking a cigarette. Her daughter, Stephanie, was strapping the brat she'd come to pick up into a stroller.

The brat was fighting and throwing a tantrum. Its fists were clenched and its top lip was caked with snot. Stephanie, short, anorexically thin, with bleached blond hair and too much make up, was ignoring it. She had the long suffering air of a mother who's resigned to this sort of behaviour.

Once the little rugrat was restrained, she left it to scream and fight against the straps while she exchanged a few words with her mother. The grey haired woman teared up as the ash dropped, unnoticed, from her cigarette. Stephanie looked a little embarrassed, but she leaned over and hugged her mother all the same, as the old bat started bawling.

Iain knew what the old hag was crying about. Her stinking son, Gavin, rotting in a holding cell, looking at twenty five years to life. As far as Iain was concerned, after what he'd done to Sandra, prison was too good for Gavin.

Sandra was Iain's sister. It had just been the two of them, in their high rise flat, since their father died. Then Gavin came along.

The police had picked him up a few streets away from their apartment.

He was drenched in Sandra's blood, raving and screaming about Iain. Gavin was on his way to find him, Iain was quite certain of that. Unlucky for Gavin then, that a neighbour called the police after the racket he'd made, and they arrived so quickly.

Sandra was found on the kitchen floor. Her throat hadn't just been cut, it had been sawn through. Her windpipe, all the muscles, tendons and arteries of her neck, had been severed, clean through to the spinal column, which was the only thing keeping the head attached to her body.

Her torso had been gutted from crotch to sternum. A knife had been placed in her genitals then forced upwards, over her pubic bone, and all the way to her rib cage, slicing through her whole stomach wall. She'd been left in a pool of congealing blood and spilled innards.

Iain had nothing but hate in his heart for Gavin. Gavin had taken something that wasn't his to take.

Stephanie wandered down to the high street, with her screaming toddler. From there, she caught a bus back to the squalid ground floor flat where she lived. Iain followed her the whole way home and parked across the road, where he could keep an eye on her through the binoculars.

Stephanie went through the same routine she'd gone through the last three nights. It hadn't changed since Iain started watching her.

She plonked the monster down in the living room. Then she'd turn on the telly and try and distract the little creature with an i-pad as well. Once the brat stopped crying and became mesmerised by the screens, Stephanie would retire to kitchen and down a whole lager in less than a minute. She took her time with the second one.

Once Stephanie was nicely oiled from the two lagers, she'd go into the living room and turn off the telly and the i-pad. The little monster would throw the mother of all tantrums.

Stephanie then went back to the kitchen for a third lager, while the brat wore itself out screaming and thrashing on the floor. It took her the same time to drink the lager, as it took the brat to wear itself out. When it had done screaming, Stephanie would pick it up, put it into pajamas and lock it in its bedroom.

Finally she'd go back into the kitchen, drink a quarter of a bottle of vodka and collapse into bed. Every night without fail. Tonight was no exception, Stephanie dragged herself off to bed in a drunken and exhausted stupor.

Matt Shaw

Not once, did it cross Stephanie's mind, that this was the last time she'd ever go through this little routine. That her short, meaningless life was about to stagger to a halt. She probably thought she had another forty years of drunkenness, motherhood and misery to look forward to. No one ever realises how close they are to murder.

When he'd made sure Stephanie was snoring through her drink induced coma, Iain turned on his engine and pulled away from the curb. He drove through the city centre and out of town. Once he was out of the suburbs, Iain turned off the main road and pulled into a hotel parking lot. A nice, remote hotel, right on the outskirts of town, perfect for what Iain had in mind. The same hotel where Stephanie worked as a chamber maid.

Iain's plan was simple. He'd booked a room over a week ago under a false name. He would spend the night, pretend to book himself out, then sneak back upstairs while Stephanie was cleaning out the rooms.

He'd surprise Stephanie with a knife, force her into one of the rooms and drag her into the bathroom. Then he'd gag her and slice her open in the exact same way that Sandra was killed. It was a simple matter of justice. Gavin had taken something that wasn't his to take. As a result, Iain no longer had his beloved sister. Tomorrow, Gavin would learn what it's like to lose a sister.

Iain was pleased to see that were no CCTV cameras anywhere in the hotel. So there'd be no record of his stay, other than a fake signature in the register. He'd cased the whole building, to make certain of this.

Iain checked his reflection in the rear view mirror, running a hand over his freshly shaved scalp. He'd dyed his beard ginger too. A pair of dark shades topped off the disguise, making him nearly unrecognisable.

Iain had the type of nondescript features that people never remembered, but there was no point taking any chances. He'd even packed a special airtight suit, that he'd bought off ebay. He was going to sleep in it tonight, then wear it while he did Stephanie. That way he wouldn't leave behind any forensic evidence. He'd watched enough CSI to know how easy it was to get caught.

Once the first part of his plan was through, Iain could move on to the second part. Stephanie's murder would be identical to Sandra's. That wouldn't just send a message to Gavin, it would also send a message to the police.

The evidence against Gavin was circumstantial at best. That's what

136

Gavin's solicitor had said on the news report. If another murder was committed, with the same MO while Gavin was in custody, then his defense could argue that both murders were the work of a serial killer. They might even try and link it to some of the recent disappearances in the area.

Either way, sooner or later Gavin was going to walk free. When he did, Iain would have him just where he wanted him. There wouldn't be any prison walls to protect him, and there'd be no bars to keep Iain out. Gavin would pay for what he did to Sandra. Gavin had taken something that wasn't his to take. Now he would learn what the consequences of that were.

Sandra didn't belong to Gavin. He had no right to do what he had done to her. The two of them, sneaking about behind everyone's backs like that, meeting up in dark alleys, or Gavin's car. What had Sandra been thinking, letting him put his hands on her body, making her sigh and moan? How could she do that to Iain, let Gavin take what rightfully belonged to *him*?

Sandra was his. Iain had never loved another woman. He'd never even touched another woman. He'd been faithful to Sandra his whole life. That's what hurt him so much, that she could betray him so coldly and callously.

Love like theirs belonged in the family and should stay in the family. It shouldn't be given away to strangers, like some cheap whore that you rented by the hour. Iain and Sandra's father had taught them that. He'd been very insistent upon it, especially after Iain's mother died.

Their mother fell from a cliff at the seaside, while they were on holiday. Iain and Sandra had seen it happen. Their father had moved so quickly, neither they, nor their mother had seen him coming. He grinned at them afterwards, as if to say: 'let that be a lesson to you'.

After that Sandra had to take on the 'wifely duties'. Their father would make Iain watch. Then he made him join in, showing him what to do, instructing him on his technique. Iain had been really scared at first. He hadn't wanted to hurt Sandra, but he was more frightened of the beating his father would give him if he had said no. He tried to make it pleasurable for Sandra. He wasn't sure she enjoyed it, but at least she didn't cry as much when it was him.

Iain had wanted to show Sandra that he could look after her. That he could spare her the beatings and the abuse. That's how their father came to die. Fell off the same cliff, only a hundred yards from where their mother had gone over the edge. He had never seen it coming either. Afterwards, Iain had grinned at Sandra. The same leering grin their father had given them. That's when he realised how much he was his father's son.

What he and Sandra had was sacred. She shouldn't have cheapened it the way she had. Iain thought she wanted it too. He was only doing what he thought was his duty by her. He still held her down, but only because he thought that's what Sandra wanted. Iain didn't know any different. He was only doing what he'd been taught.

He couldn't believe it when he caught her packing her suitcase. After everything Iain had done to keep the family together, to keep Sandra safe. That was how she repaid him.

She tried to talk to him of course, pretending to reason with him so she could get him out of the way long enough to escape. She told Iain that she still loved him. But how could she love him if she was betraying him like that?

Iain hadn't expected Gavin to call when he had. He'd gone out to the shops to get a tarpaulin and a load of cleaning products. Sandra must have given him a key or something. He might even have been calling by to pick her up and take her away from Iain.

He hadn't expected the police to arrive so quickly and take Gavin away from him either. He had been planning on visiting Gavin next, but Gavin had turned up at the wrong time and ruined Iain's first plan. Not that it had mattered in the long run, Iain had a new plan and Gavin would still pay. Gavin had taken something that wasn't his to take - Sandra's love. He would pay dearly for that. Just as Sandra had paid, when Iain severed her throat and gutted her.

Iain got his bags out of the car and walked to reception. The girl behind the counter smiled at him. Stupid cow. She had no idea of the atrocities that were going to take place under the roof of that hotel next morning.

She was oblivious to it all. She'd carry on with all her little duties and never have a clue what was going on right under her nose. Like he always said. *No one ever realises how close they are to murder.*

Part Five

THE
FINAL NIGHT

Chapter One

I dragged what was left of Christie's body over to the furnace. I'm still not sure what I am going to be doing with my life after tonight and - in all honesty - it stresses me out to try and think about it. For once there is no long-term plan. *For once?* Was this hotel ever a long-term plan? Truth be told I am surprised I managed to get away with it for as long as I have. Here I am, feeling blue, that it could be coming to an end and yet... I've achieved so much. There is nothing to feel melancholy about. If anything I should be feeling proud of what I have done.

I looked down at the woman's abused body. Broken. Twisted. Dead. I'm not sure how many of these there have been but I'm sure, had I been counting, I would have been one of the country's leading serial killers. Something else to feel proud about.

I sighed.

Why do I always do this to myself?

I have my fun and then - after - I beat myself up, putting myself down. Woe is me. I sound pathetic to those who would hear me. I looked back down at the body. Do you hear me? I laughed at the thought of being judged by a corpse. Fuck you.

I bent down and scooped the body up. Without a further word, I tipped it into the furnace. She landed on Duncan's burning body and immediately the flames started licking her flesh away. Goodbye my love. Sweet dreams and all that jazz.

As I watched the bodies burn, I thought back to our time together. There was no doubt about it, we had fun. I made him cut his own balls off and eat them… He was forced to cut her pussy out of her body and make himself a little fuck-glove… Admittedly some bits worked better than other ideas but it was still fun experimenting with what was possible and what wasn't. In hindsight, I should have made him cut a fuck-glove from her cunt to masturbate with before making him cut his own balls off. Watching him stick a flaccid, bloody dick into her bloody pulp… Didn't really work as well as I had imagined it would. Oh well. We live and learn.

I grabbed a metal pole from where it leaned against the wall and - standing back - I pushed the furnace door shut with it. The next time I open the door, the two bodies will be more or less gone. That's the end of their story. Actually… Maybe not. The camera we'd filmed with caught my eye from across the room, where I had left it on the side. Their story doesn't end. Their story will live on for as long as the tape does. Hard to forget those gone when you can relive their mannerisms, and the sound of their voices, through film. A busy night ahead of me but… Always time to have a quick look to see what the footage looks like. I smiled to myself. I can spare a couple of minutes.

Leaving the bodies to be consumed by the fires, I crossed the room and made a grab for the camera. It won't take long to wire everything into the television in my office and it will take even less time to actually *enjoy* the footage… A couple of minutes I can definitely spare before the night *really* gets going.

Still smiling, I headed up the stairs and back towards the foyer of my hotel. A part of me wondered, as I neared the top step, what would happen to it once I was gone? Would the hotel remain open and be taken over by someone else? Someone who would find the many secrets? Would it be demolished when the truth came to light? Or would it remain open but transformed to a museum for the crimes committed? I like that idea and - given the world we live in - there is definitely money to be made there.

Everyone likes horror. Even more so if you pretend the building is haunted with the ghosts of those who died there. People believe absolutely anything these days and everyone likes a ghost story.

*

I turned into the foyer to the sound of someone banging the front door.

'Open the door! Open the fucking door!'

I recognised the man who Agata had checked in a few days ago. He looks better now than he had back when he had signed the paperwork for the room. Pete. If memory serves correctly - and it usually does - that is his name.

'You!' He had spotted me standing in the doorway watching him. 'Open the door. I have to leave...'

'Terribly sorry, it's our policy to lock the door after a certain hour. If you bear with me, I'll get the key for you.' He looked panicked. His face was white as a sheet almost as though - funnily enough - he had seen a ghost himself. I kept the conversation going as I walked over to the reception area, if anything to stop him from rattling the damned doors, 'Is everything okay, sir?' I asked. I don't really care.

He started to cry. Quite a pathetic sight.

'She's dead,' he muttered at first. Then, louder, 'She's fucking dead!'

My heart skipped a beat. What had he seen?

'I have to tell the police...'

'Sir, calm down, I'm sure it's not what you think it is...'

'Don't you fucking tell me to calm down! I watched...'

Had someone been watching me? Had he found one of my spy-holes and happened to look through it at the wrong time? I felt a sickness swirling in the pit of my stomach. No, he couldn't have. Everyone is locked in their rooms, he couldn't have stumbled onto one of the spy-holes... What am I saying? If he had been locked in his room, he wouldn't be here now.

I set the camera down on the reception desk.

'If you wait right here, sir, I just need to get the key from my office.'

I walked from the foyer into the back office. He continued to shout that she was dead, over and over again like a broken record. In the office, I grabbed a sharp knife from the top drawer of my desk. I'm glad the majority of the main rooms are sound-proofed. It would make my night a lot harder if people could hear him ranting and raving down here. They'd all likely try to come from their rooms to investigate the noise.

With the knife held behind my back, I walked back into the foyer with the office door slamming shut behind me.

'She's fucking dead and I could have stopped it.'

I smiled. He wasn't the biggest of men. 'I doubt you could have.'

'I just watched as they killed her. It's my fault,' he wept.

I stopped in my tracks. Wait? What? I asked the question, 'What are you talking about? Who's dead? Who killed who?'

He stopped pacing and suddenly stared at something behind me.

'I'm sorry,' he said.

'No need to apologise. What happened?' I continued, 'Maybe I can help?' And - then - I realised he wasn't apologising to me. He was looking through me. Puzzled, I turned. No one was standing there. I turned back to him.

'Please - open the door... I have to go to the police,' he said again.

I nodded. 'It's okay. Whatever happened I'm sure it will all be okay.'

'Fuck you! Don't tell me everything will be okay! They fucking burned her! They set her on fire and...' He started to cry again. 'I loved her. I would have looked after her... I would have...'

'They killed someone you love?' I asked.

He nodded.

'The person you love is dead.' I walked across the foyer to him. 'It's really not that bad a deal.'

'They killed her,' he said again quietly, almost to himself.

'And I killed *you* and now, quite sweet really, the two of you are together...'

He looked at me, puzzled. Before he had a chance for a further reaction, I revealed the knife and slashed it across the width of his throat. He fell back against the door as a jettison of blood sprayed over my face and the floor. I grinned, the taste of iron in my mouth, as he slid down the door down onto the hard, cold tiles - his hands pressed to his throat. I tossed the knife to one side and crouched down next to him.

'The person you love is dead,' I told him, staring him in the eye. 'Why are you trying to fight this?' I moved his hands away from his throat. He had no fight in him. The blood wasn't flowing half as much as when I made the initial cut. Won't be long now. He turned away from me and stared to the side. Suddenly - a smile on his face. What's that about? He mouthed something that I couldn't understand and then, his whole body relaxed. A final sigh from his mouth.

I sat there a moment, unsure what the hell had just happened. I've had people scream before but... Makes me realise, I know very little about the guests who come through the doors, only their name and - even then - I'm sure, sometimes, they don't leave their real details. Looking at his dead body, I can't help but wonder what his story was. A split second later, I realise I don't actually care. I often wonder who these people are in their day to day life. I imagine them doing this and that and picturing what they're like with their family but - honestly - I prefer killing them. Besides, right now... I have a video tape to watch...

Chapter Two

Static on screen, flaccid penis in hand. The fun I had had making that film and - yet - it failed to hit the spot, even using the lobby man's blood - wiped from my face - as a warm lubricant to increase my sought after pleasure. Admittedly I had fast forwarded the way through the film in nothing more than a few minutes, just to find the good stuff but even so, I can't hide the feeling of disappointment that I feel as I sit back in the chair. Erotic to film, boring to view. Fuck sake, even the security footage of me drowning that fucker in the toilet of his en-suite... Even watching him choke on his fresh turd, glugging down the yellow water, was more erotic than this crap. I feel a disappointment which will be redirected towards one of the unfortunate guests left in the hotel. I get disappointed, they suffer. Those are the rules that I put in place. Rules that they get no say in.

Leaving the cable in the back of the television, I reached for the controller on the side and flicked the channels back to the security camera feed. All my little guests, tucked up in their beds or sitting around in their rooms. All of them feeling safe and secure here. I get disappointed, they suffer. *Those are the rules.*

I settle on one of the rooms on the first floor. An old man is in his bed sleeping. A quick cross-reference between the captured room and the list of guests noted - in the system's electronic file - and his name is Desmond. He looks peaceful there. A happy customer tucked up safe and sound in their rented bed. How sweet. How serene. I laughed to myself as I reached for a wireless keyboard. He doesn't know it yet but he is one of the lucky ones. He gets a peaceful exit that most of us yearn for; to pass away in our sleep.

I leaned forward in my chair and pressed a key on the computer's keyboard. I sat back and waited. Only a subtle change happens in Desmond's room - one that can't be seen on screen immediately. The vents of the air-conditioning unit have sealed shut. A second later and an invisible gap starts to pump into the room from canisters stored in the dead-space between his room and the next. One of the many fun little traps I've installed in the hotel.

'Goodnight, Desmond.' I muttered under my breath as I watched him stir. He didn't wake up, just twisted in the duvet a little as though his brain was *trying* to warn him there was a problem. With the speed the gas pumps into the room, it won't be long before he is suffocated. I smiled as I felt a twitch in my cock. It doesn't take much to please me and the traps in the hotel... They always hit the spot. Well, almost always. Ida was definitely a disappointment - so much so that she had almost slipped my mind. Scary considering it only happened earlier today...

To be continued.

Interval

HIDDEN SURPRISES

...Earlier

Usually they're panicking by now. They've tried getting out of the locked door, they've attempted to push the wall as it continues to close in on them, threatening to crush them, they've tried screaming, they're tried putting furniture in the centre of the room to try and stop the advancing walls... Nothing ever works. The last thing they do is to stand in the centre of the boxed-room and panic. Some of them - whilst panicking - scream, some of them pray, some... Some try and make calls on their phones, no doubt to loved ones. Calls that never go through thanks to the signal blocker I use. This woman though - Ida Wells according to the guest book... She isn't doing anything. She is just sitting in the centre of the room. There's a look on her bruised, battered face which suggests she has simply given up. Given up? Of all the guests I have seen enter this room, I have never seen anyone just give up like this. They always have some fight left in them, right until the four walls meet and they get squashed - flattened to such a state they no longer appear human in form. Just a puddle of bone powder and gore.

I lean forward to a microphone, plugged into my system. A press of the little red button on the microphone's stand and I can talk directly to the occupant of the room.

'The walls will not stop until you're crushed,' I say quietly.

Ida, down on her knees, didn't react to my voice or the words I said. Other people, in a similar position, have screamed for me to let them out. They're screams I ignore but I'm finding it frustrating that she isn't playing ball. I ignore them, but I enjoy them.

I continued, 'It's a painful death. You can feel your bones break and your organs rupture. Even feel as your eyeballs are squeezed from their sockets. A painful death,' I reiterated.

Ida had been sleeping before I activated the walls. A sleep disturbed with the heavy creaking as the walls started closing in around her. A quick death to satisfy my need as I plan what to do with Agata. More than that - a quick death before this woman causes me problems. I saw her come into the hotel, face bent out of shape. I don't want trouble here and all the time she is here, under my roof, she has the potential to bring it - whether on purpose or by accident. I can't allow that - not when it can lead to investigation from authorities if things get out of hand. It wouldn't be the first time I have had a rowdy guest bring a visit from the police. I got away with it that time, but I doubt I would get it away with it for a second time. Can't keep pushing my luck. Even after what I'd said to her - she still doesn't seem to be concerned.

I frowned.

'Do you want to die?' I asked into the microphone.

On screen she shrugged. 'Maybe I deserve it?' she said - her voice picked up by a small microphone built into the speaker integrated into the ceiling. The camera cut out as the wall passed by where it was built into the ceiling, close to the microphone and speaker. She doesn't have long left now.

I sat back in my chair and awaited the screams. She might be putting on a brave face now but - when death is moments away - they always scream.

I waited, listening carefully. To my surprise there was no sound of screaming. There was only the sound of bones crunching and - then - the walls, finally, coming together.

I do not need to press a button to have the walls go back to their original positioning. It happens automatically after five minutes. On the off-chance the person is still alive (never yet happened) the pressure of the walls closed will be enough to suffocate them slowly. Like I said, though, it's never happened before. When the walls shut, they shut good and proper - nice and tight and the people trapped within are turned to nothing but a puddle of shit. Even so, though, no rush getting the walls to open again. I've found that it is easier to clean the mess up if the blood has a chance to dry on the walls. Open them too fast and it will just run down onto the floor and there will be more to clean.

I reached for my hot drink - one of the last tasks I had Agata do for me before it became her turn to see the person I truly am. It's lukewarm now but I still find myself sipping it as though it was still boiling hot. I sit back and sigh. I can't help but feel a little deflated by the lack of this bitch's scream. I take little comfort in the fact she still would have suffered, even if she did do it in silence. Her pain was still very real. Little comfort is better than zero comfort, I suppose, and I can always make Agata suffer double to make up for it.

A thought enters my head, *maybe I should have the walls close a little slower? If it's slower - they suffer more.* An easy fix and one I can do later in the week if I choose to. Maybe then she would have screamed?

Why didn't the cunt scream? What could have been so bad in her life that she could just give up like that and welcome not only the pain but the cold grip of death too?

What kind of mental case was she? I shrugged. I'll never know.

*

Ida Wells
(Women's MMA Welterweight #1 Contender)
by
Wrath James White

Ida stared out the window as the taxi cruised down the empty streets, navigating the sparse evening traffic. She had an ice pack pressed against her swollen jaw. The city was desolate, a funereal silence pressed in on all sides from the shadowy streets. They passed the occasional bustling bar or nightclub, but, for the most part, the streets were completely dead. This city was nothing like San Francisco. At one o'clock in the morning on a Saturday night, there would have been people on every corner. Most of her friends didn't even leave the house until after ten pm on the weekends.

Her cell phone vibrated in her pocket again. It had been going off every few minutes since she'd left the arena. It was either her manager or her trainer or both. She wasn't in the mood to talk. They passed a billboard with her face on it and Ida grit her teeth against the bad taste it left in her mouth. She looked like a serious bad-ass in that photo, with her buzz-cut blonde hair, and steely blue eyes, her hard, muscular physique. She looked unstoppable. People were always surprised when they met her in person and saw how small she was. Ida was only five-feet-five inches tall and weighed less than a hundred and forty pounds. That's what a welterweight is, but fans always expected her to be bigger because she looked so formidable in her photos. Ida hoped they took all those posters and signs down soon. Now that it was over, she just wanted to forget.

'This one right here is fine,' Ida said, and the taxi pulled to a stop in front of a liquor store.

'Are you sure? This isn't the best place for a lady to be alone at night. It gets kinda seedy downtown once all the businesses close. I mean, I know you can take care of yourself, but still.'

'Thanks, but I'll be fine.'

Ida stepped out of the taxi. Her clothes were still sweaty. She hadn't bothered taking a shower after the fight. She had just wanted to get out of there. After peeling out of her fight gear, she'd dressed quickly and hurried out of the arena, still angry, livid bruises on her face, busted lip, bleeding knuckles, and a limp she was trying to hide out of embarrassment. Everyone was probably wondering where she'd gone, afraid that she was going to do something stupid like go see her ex-fiance. But Ida wasn't feeling quite that self-destructive.

She wore sunglasses though the sun was still several hours from rising. It was a barrier between her and the rest of the world. Ida wanted to climb into a dark, quiet, corner and hide, and the sunglasses made all the corners dark. They allowed her to pretend that no one could see her, because she couldn't see them.

'It happens to the best of them ...'

The taxi driver was saying something to her.

'Huh? What?'

'I'm serious. It was a great fight. I really thought you fought well. I mean, you did your best, right? That's all that counts,' The taxi driver said.

Was that what everyone would think? That I did my best? Would people think that shitty performance was all I had in me? That was even more depressing than if people thought she had choked. Ida knew in her heart that she was capable of so much more than the half-ass effort she'd put forth tonight. So much more.

'You'll be back. You'll get her next time.'

Ida thought she detected an Italian accent, though it could have been Spanish or Portugese. The driver's dark, curly hair and ruddy complexion could have placed him as any number of different nationalities. The identification card on his dashboard said Michael Anthony. The name could not have been more generic had it been John Smith.

'Thanks for trying to cheer me up, but I got my ass kicked,' Ida said, handing the driver the cab fare she owed along with a generous tip for his kind-hearted lie. She dumped her ice pack into a trash can and spit a wad of bloody phlegm onto the sidewalk.

'Hey, at least you never tapped. You went out on your shield like a true warrior. There's honor in that. You should be proud.'

The driver was saying all the things you were supposed to say to someone when they lost. It was exactly what her trainer would have said. That's why she didn't want to answer the phone. She didn't want to hear it. It wasn't necessary. She could do his end of the conversation. Ida felt tears well up. She faked a smile, nodded, then quickly turned away and headed toward the liquor store.

'You want me to wait for you?'

'No, you go ahead. I'll catch another cab later. Thanks.'

'You sure? I can wait.'

Ida didn't reply. She walked into the liquor store and headed straight for the tequila.

She hoped the driver was right, and she'd get another shot. This had been her dream for the last four years, ever since she made the switch from boxing to mixed martial arts. She had been one of the most highly touted prospects in the history of the sport. It wasn't every day that an Olympic boxer steps into the cage. But, after such a poor performance, she had her doubts that she'd ever get another shot.

I looked like shit out there — in front of the whole world! I let that bitch punk me!

This had been her one big chance, the fight of a lifetime, a championship fight for the women's welterweight mixed martial arts world title, on national TV, and she had blown it, let personal shit get in the way. Ida was sure she'd drop so low in the ranking now that it would take her years to fight her way back into contention. Years fighting the toughest, hungriest young prospects the match-makers could throw at her, and if she lost to any of them, that would be the end of her title aspirations. It sucked, because she knew in her heart that she could have won.

I knew I shouldn't have gotten involved with that bitch, Ida thought. *The pretty ones fuck you over every time.*

But Lisa was supposed to be different. She was so sweet and innocent, not like the butch leather dykes Ida usually dated. But, just two weeks before the fight, she'd walked in on Lisa in their apartment with the neighbor's cock halfway down her throat and she'd gone berserk. She broke the guy's arm and knocked him unconscious then beat Lisa to within an inch of her life. The police had come and Ida spent the next two days in jail before her manager bailed her out. Those last days leading up to the fight she hadn't gone to the gym once. She'd spent every night in the bar getting drunk and picking up chicks. It was the only way she knew how to cope, drown the memory of Lisa in pussy and alcohol.

'Is that all, Miss?'

'What?'

'The tequila? Is that all?'

'Uh, yeah. This is all I need,' Ida replied, stroking the bottle sensuously, like she was preparing to make love to it.

'I'll need to see some identification,' the store clerk said. He was a young freckle-faced boy, probably just barely old enough to purchase alcohol himself.

Ida fished in the pocket of her jogging pants and pulled out her wallet, then handed over her driver's license, bracing for the humiliating moment when she would be recognized. Just two weeks ago, she'd loved meeting fans, signing autographs, answering questions about her training techniques, fight strategy, and future plans. Now, she craved anonymity.

'I can't see your face with those glasses on.'

'Are you fucking kidding me?'

'I'm sorry, ma'am. State law.'

Grimacing, Ida slowly removed her sunglasses. She caught the clerk's horrified expression when he saw her swollen eyes and bruised face. She rolled her eyes, waiting for the questions to come.

'Whoa! Are you okay, Ma'am?'

'Just ring up the damn tequila so I can go home and get drunk,' Ida said, then winced internally when she remembered she no longer had a home to go to. The apartment had been in Lisa's name. She was homeless.

The clerk handed her back her ID, and scanned the tequila.

'Twelve dollars.'

Ida handed him a twenty and waited uncomfortably for him to make change. He kept casting glances at her face. His mouth opened and shut several times, but no words came out, and Ida realized he probably thought she was a battered wife or something and was trying to find the proper words to convince her to get help.

'You know, there are places you can go – '

'Save it,' Ida replied.

'I mean, whoever did this to you – '

'I'm a fighter. I get paid to look like this,' Ida said, then snatched the tequila off the counter and stormed out the door. She knew the kid was just trying to do the right thing, be a good citizen, but she had still felt like punching him in his mouth. She knew she could have made his face look so much worse than hers did. Let him be the one dealing with other people's bullshit sympathy. But that would have made her the asshole, which would have only made her feel worse.

The only positive thing about the evening was that her fight had taken place at a casino, and she had been able to cash her twenty-thousand-dollar check right there on the spot, at almost midnight. Walking around the streets at one am with twenty grand in her pocket probably wasn't smart, but Ida didn't really feel like being smart tonight. Being smart was the very last thing Ida wanted to be. Right now, what she wanted to do most was get so drunk she would lose all sense of responsibility, and do something reckless, impulsive, and preferably violent. But Ida could feel her rage and adrenaline fueled energy beginning to ebb. In the wake of her waning anger, she felt tired, lonely, heartbroken, and defeated, utterly and thoroughly defeated. She unscrewed the cap off the tequila and took a big gulp that burned its way down her throat into her belly. Her eyes watered up, and she wasn't sure if it was from the tequila or her fucked up life.

Ida remembered seeing a building on the corner a few blocks down that had a 'rooms for rent' sign on it. She didn't know if anyone would be awake at this hour, but she had nowhere else to go. If no one answered the door, she'd sleep in the building's doorway until morning.

Ida took another long swig from the tequila bottle, then began to stumble down the street in the direction of the big building. All she remembered was that there had been a restaurant and a pharmacy on the ground floor, and the rest of the building had looked like a fancy hotel. She'd passed it in the taxi on her way to the liquor store, so it couldn't have been very far.

Her left thigh hurt like hell from where she'd taken repeated leg kicks. Everything hurt. From the inside out. Her muscles felt weak, dried out. As she stumbled along, her thoughts bounced from memories of the fight, the punches she's missed, the kicks she'd taken, and finally being choked unconscious, waking up with the referee standing above her, to the expression on Lisa's face when she'd walked in to find her down on her knees with her head bobbing up and down in the neighbor's lap. Ida screamed and punched her already bruised fist against a store window. The window didn't break, but it felt like her hand would.

She pulled out her phone and scanned through the messages. She had sixty-six missed calls and fourteen text messages. There was one there from

Lisa. She opened it.

'I know you hate me right now, but I forgive you for hitting me. I mean, I shouldn't. But I do. The doctor's said I almost lost an eye. You gave me a concussion and two broken ribs. But I still love you. I forgive you. Why can't you forgive me? I fucked up, but you need someone in your corner right now. Just call me back, and tell me you're okay.'

Ida considered deleting the message. Instead, she threw the phone across the street. It struck a light post and shattered into pieces. The effort made her feel even more exhausted. Tears flowed freely down her face. She wiped them away with one hand while raising the tequila bottle to her lips with the other.

Fuck this night. I just want it to end.

She could see the building just a half a block away now. It was closer than she'd remembered.

*

Just another example of how all my guests have their own little stories. Not that I'll ever know what they were. Not that I actually *care*.

Setting the drink to one side, I leaned forward and killed the computer screen before picking up the telephone sitting to the side of the monitor. I dialled through to the reception desk.

'Hi, Agata, just wondered if you were ready to check out the cellar?'

I smiled as she answered.

'That's great,' I continued, 'I'm on my way.'

Ida didn't scream. Agata will.

Part Five

THE
FINAL NIGHT
(continued)

Matt Shaw

Chapter Three

Desmond would be dead by now. It never takes long. Not that I'm in a hurry to turn the gas off. Leave it on to be one hundred percent sure and - then - when I am ready, open the vents again and get it pumped from the room before I go in to move his body to the trapdoor in the secret corridor. Mind you, I still go in wearing a gas mask just to be on the safe side. The last thing I needed would be to go in and collapse thanks to the fumes. Imagine, the pair of us being found by a passer-by. An embarrassing way to go for sure. I would look like an amateur and - that I'm not. Amateurs make mistakes. I don't. Everything is planned meticulously and...

My heart skipped a beat and I twisted to the closed office door at the sound of smashing glass coming from beyond, out in the main foyer. *What the fuck was that?* I swivelled in the chair back to the computer and leaned forward to the keyboard. A quick press of the escape button and Desmond's death scene minimises, allowing me to see various angles of the hotel captured by the hidden cameras. A simple click and the foyer fills the screen. My heart is still pounding - throbbing in the back of my throat - as I see a girl and boy running around the foyer. The boy was standing by the broken window of the hotel doors, a few feet from the body of the man whose throat I had slit. The girl was over by the reception desk, standing next to the computer. Another one of my guests - the vicar - is standing on the stairs - clear panic on his face too. What the hell? Why are they all out of their rooms? They were locked in... At least, I thought they were.

I jumped up and hurried across the office floor over to the door. I thought they were locked away. I should have made sure. Or - at the very least - cleared away the body from the foyer. A clumsy, silly mistake that I would never usually make. I opened the door and...

First the pain hit me. A heavy slog to the chest.

Then I registered her scream.

And the sound of the gun shot ringing through the air.

I fell back into the office and landed flat on my back. Lying there, the pain burning through my body now, I looked down to my stomach as blood seeped through my white shirt. I looked past my own body and out of the office door into the foyer. The girl was standing there with a smoking gun in her hand.

The Reverend, Vicar... Whatever the fuck he is, yelled from the stairs as the girl dropped the gun to the floor. 'What is going on?'

'We saw it, man...' The lad from by the door replied, 'This motherfucker cut this guy's throat as though he were nothing and then disappeared into his office. We were trying to get out but the door is electronically locked. Grace was trying to unlock it from the computer when I thought it better to just smash the fucking thing and make a run for it... This cunt...'

She must have released the locks for the other rooms. Would explain how the vicar came to be about...

'He scared me,' the girl said as my vision blurred. 'I wasn't expecting him to come out of the office like that... I didn't mean to...'

'You poor girl, come here...' As the man of God approached the girl, his arms outstretched to offer a protective embrace, my head dropped back down onto the carpeted floor. The pain in my stomach screaming. It hurts too much to hold my head up.

'Grace,' the other man shouted, 'come on... Let's just get the fuck out of here... We don't need to be a part of this...'

I heard footsteps on broken glass as they fled, leaving the vicar standing dumbstruck. At least, I presume they are fleeing... Staring up at the ceiling, I couldn't help but let out a small sigh - almost a little laugh... My mind has drifted back to Jonathan - the young man who had been making a habit of killing the homeless men... Had I recruited him... Had I let him in on my hobby... Things would have ended differently. We would have been ending this evening as I had initially planned; killing everyone in this God forsaken hotel. Now...

The Vicar came into my view. He looked down at me, with pity in his eyes. He smiled at me. I'm not sure if it's a smile of comfort or…

'God forgives,' he said.

I want to answer him. I want to ask him if he believes that because he needs to be forgiven but I can't answer. The pain is unbearable in my stomach and yet the rest of my body feels cold and numb…

In my mind, I see Jonathan sneak up behind him and placing a knife against the back of his neck.

I hear Jonathan say, 'There is no God.' And - with that - the vicar's eyes bulge as the tip of the blade pushes through his spine and penetrates his windpipe. As I die, I listen to the vicar choke on his own blood. It's music to my ears.

I imagine Jonathan standing over me. Soft words whispered that everything is going to be okay. He knows someone that can help fix me up and that I shouldn't worry. Everything will be all right. We'll leave this place… We'll set up another place to work from in another country… Maybe keep the same name? Maybe call it something new? Everything will be fine, I just need to trust him. I smile. How do you trust a murderer? A fleeting thought as I imagine a new place and a new way to work… The hiring of more people like Jonathan where I no longer need to stress about staff discovering my secret or guests stumbling into the violence unexpected… A place where we can kill together… I groan in pain.

The pain and suffering I've caused others… I always thought I would have died in a more fitting manner and yet… I get off relatively light. No such thing as bad Karma then…

My vision fades, as does my consciousness.

Matt Shaw

Part Six

DREAMS
OF A
DYING MAN

Matt Shaw

The Grande Hotel.
What Could Have Been

by

Mark Tufo

'Aah...Jenner. Almost on time for your very first day!' Henry said, a huge smile splitting his face from ear to ear. He was a tall man, nearly six and a half feet, but he was gaunt. He always wore the same jovial expression, a strange contrast to his perpetually gray, sickly pallor. Henry once had designs on becoming a doctor, but when his older brother, George, had died suddenly, he became the sole inheritor of the Grande. It had been in his family for four generations and his parents would not take 'no' for an answer. Though the circumstances of George's death were suspicious, the lawyers finally gave in and Henry began his life as a hotelier.

'Sorry, Mr. Henry. I could not find my dress shoes,' Jenner said sheepishly. He prided himself on his grasp of the English language. He'd come over from Warsaw, not two months previously, but he'd studied laboriously the language of the world before he made his journey. It was his hope that he would do well enough in his new job to be able to send for the woman he loved. Paulina, he knew, would embrace this opulent life.

'That is all you have?' Henry asked as he gazed upon two old and frayed travel bags.

'It is, Mr. Henry.'

Henry looked around. Matilda and her housekeeping staff would not be up and about for another hour or so and he himself was watching the front desk, having given Derrick Kowalski, the night clerk, the evening off. Henry pulled a handkerchief from his pocket and wiped away the beads of sweat that had formed on his brow.

'Come, come. Let's get you a room to stay in. And perhaps we can find you some shoes. I cannot allow you to greet our guests in—*tennis shoes.*' Henry nearly spat out those last words. 'I don't understand where fashion has gone. The world dressed well in my parents' day. People took pride in their appearance. This hotel has welcomed many beautiful patrons.'

'Yes, Mr. Henry,' Jenner said nervously. He'd obviously upset his new boss; a terrible beginning, but he would make it up to him by showing how hard he could work. This position paid well; one of the better salaries for a young man of little skill. And the benefit of free room and board! It was unheard of. Yes, if he managed his earnings correctly, his beloved could be with him by the end of the year.

Henry escorted his new staff member to the elevator and put his hand out to let him enter first. Before stepping in himself, Henry looked up and down both sides of the hallway, then let the doors close behind him. He pressed the fifth-floor button, clasped his long, gray hands in front of him, and stared straight forward. Jenner got his first real look at just how tall his new boss was as he stood next to him, and slightly forward. Neither man said anything for the short ride up, but Jenner could not help but steal glances at Henry. His thinning hair was neatly slicked back; his skin looked as if it hadn't seen the sun in years. His formal attire was an older style, but well kept; very clean. His shoulders stooped forward like so many tall men who grow accustomed to looking down on their company. Jenner smiled to himself, thinking Henry looked like a stereotypical butler in a Hollywood horror movie. That smile turned abruptly to a grimace when he saw movement on Henry's neck, just at his hairline. Tiny, translucent worms wriggled about looking for hairs to clasp where they could eat and lay eggs to their heart's content. Jenner quietly sidestepped away, fearing offending his boss, but not wanting to get any of the lice on him. Henry absently scratched at the back of his neck. Jenner watched in abject disgust as five of the parasites fell to the floor and began to wriggle their way towards his shoe.

Jenner thought it odd when Henry blocked the exit to look again down the hallway both ways before letting him off, but he chalked it up to caution; his boss must be trying to avoid accidents with guests, though he seemed rather anxious about it.

'Five-sixteen. This is your new home away from home,' Henry mumbled barely audibly as he opened the door quickly and nearly shoved Jenner through before once again taking a nervous glance down the hallway. When he was convinced he'd not been seen, he shut the door and turned the lock. Jenner took no notice. He was busy looking with pride at his surroundings. It was a small but clean room, and it was all his. There was a queen sized bed against the far wall, next to it sat a night table adorned by a lamp. A writing desk with a leather swivel chair was off in the corner, and a six drawer dresser with a small television sitting atop was directly in front of the bed. To his immediate left was a minuscule bathroom, done in white subway tiles, their grout yellowed with age.

Jenner's eyes traveled back to a welcome basket perched on the writing desk; he could see two bottles of water and wrapped bread goods. It was then his stomach reminded him he'd yet to eat this morning.

Henry clapped him on the shoulder and laughed. 'Sounds like you might be a little hungry. By all means, unpack, get comfortable, eat something. I'll check on those shoes. Sometimes guests leave things behind...I have four boxes of unclaimed items. I'm sure we can find something for you—what are you? About a nine?'

'Ten, sir.'

'I'll be back in an hour or so to show you the ropes.'

'Thank you again for the opportunity, sir.'

'Oh, Jenner,' he smiled vaguely. 'It should be I thanking you.' And with that, Henry unlatched the door and left the room. Jenner could only be confused by that response, the subtleties of the language were still difficult. He would have dwelled on it further if his gurgling stomach hadn't so rudely interrupted him.

He rooted around the basket, pulling out a cherry Pop-Tart, his absolute favorite, he'd nearly finished the first square before he twisted the top off his bottled water. He'd been in such a rush to wash down his breakfast he hadn't noticed that the safety seal had previously been broken, nor did he notice the slightly metallic taste as it mixed with the sickeningly sweet pastry. He finished the second tart in record time. 'I think I'm going to like it here,' he said as he took another sip, set the bottle down, then dumped his bags on the bed. As he kicked his beat-up shoes across the floor, his head swam; he steadied himself on the dresser, pulled open the top drawer, and began putting items in, barely aware of what he was doing.

2

Henry, once he left Jenner's room, went two doors down to the supply closet. He looked both ways, inserted a key from a large cluster, walked in, and closed the door behind him, leaving him in total darkness. It was a tight fit until he hit the hidden latch under the utility sink. With a soft click, a secret door opened up behind shelves full of cleaning supplies. He entered and quietly shut the shelf-lined door behind him. The narrow corridor was inky black, but he'd traversed the way enough times that he could have done it blindfolded. Henry preferred the darkness; he used to have small peepholes drilled through the walls, pinpoints of light which lined the corridor. But one evening, Wanda, his former Concierge, tipped over her lamp which had hit the picture on the wall, and knocked it askew. Wanda had seen the hole.

She ran to his office, worried that someone had been spying on her. She was so upset, so…beautifully distressed. He had gone back up to the room with her immediately so they could investigate together. To this day he still savored every sweet moment he'd had with her, though he was sure she wouldn't see it that way. He missed Wanda; she was a wonderful woman, and a capable concierge. She just had a tendency to make poor decisions. After that near discovery he had spackled every peephole and installed small wireless video cameras in the television sets, successfully moving the Droiture into the twenty-first century. With his trusty iPad, he was able to dial in any one of the fifty-seven rooms in the hotel. Right now, he was solely focused on one Jenner Greatine, a young man that, apparently, could neither be on time nor properly attired for his very first day of work. But he would pay. He would pay terribly for his transgressions.

'You're going to make me forget all about Wanda,' Henry said soothingly as he connected to the camera in room five sixteen. Jenner was putting some of his things away, stuffing socks in the dresser, hanging shirts in the closet and occasionally stopping to take a few bites from his impromptu breakfast. 'That's right, bigger drinks…ummm. That's good isn't it?' Henry's left hand traced the line of the growing bulge through his pants. He stopped when he heard the voice of his mother scolding him for being a disgusting little boy. He still felt the pain from the time she'd made him walk around with a sprung mousetrap attached to his penis for almost an hour. She slowly and deliberately opened it once half of his length had turned a vicious shade of purple, verging on black.

Threatening to let the steel wire snap back she said, 'You ever touch your disgusting little worm for anything other than going to the bathroom and I'll pull it off and feed it to the street cats!' She'd warned him, and he fully believed her. He had been only six, wholly unaware of what was so bad about touching any part of himself.

'Momma,' he'd asked, terrified and confused, 'why would God put something on my body that I can't touch?'

'The devil put that there!' She'd punctuated her point by backhanding him to the ground. 'Women are God's creatures; only men have been given that dangling curse!'

'Yes, momma.' Henry said as he once again gyrated against his hand. He watched as Jenner pushed his clothing aside and flopped onto the bed, his eyelids becoming irresistibly heavy. Suddenly a nap seemed like the best thing in the world. 'Sleep…that's right, sleep,' Henry told him quietly. Within minutes Jenner had fallen into a drugged slumber. Henry knew from experience there was nothing on earth that could wake the man, save time—a good long amount of it, as a matter of fact. Five hours was more than enough to gain access to his room through the small closet and do whatever he pleased. He entered silently, accessing a perfectly flat, hinged panel. He ducked under the hanger rod and pushed past Jenner's meager belongings. Henry pulled up the chair and sat, staring at Jenner's sleeping form, again absently stroking his penis. It wasn't that he was attracted to Jenner—or any human, as a matter of fact—it was the delightfully naughty thoughts of what he was going to do to his charge that had him so aroused.

After twenty minutes or so, Henry stood. He packed up Jenner's things and placed them through the closet and into the secret corridor. When that was done, he went back and tenderly swept the hair from Jenner's face, then gently lifted the other man as if he weighed no more than a rag doll. He'd return to the room later to make sure there was no trace of Jenner ever having been there, but for right now, it was important that Jenner be set-up in his new accommodations. Henry kicked the small panel closed, stepped over the two bags, and walked the fifty feet to the staircase at the end of the corridor. Without hesitation or misstep, he descended deeper into the bowels of the hotel, three floors below the front entrance. He loved that these old buildings were carved right into the earth and lined with heavy, solid ledge rocks; it kept even the most throat-shredding screams from reaching any of his guests or staff. And he needed that sound; it assured him he was succeeding in his discipline.

3

Jenner felt like he had the morning after he'd drunk his cousin Belenko's homemade wine. His head throbbed and his throat was parched dry. It wasn't until he tried to move his arms that fear began to clear-cut through his haze.

'I like to be here when my employees awake,' Henry said. He was in a chair some five feet away, a book in his lap. Jenner craned his neck but couldn't see the man properly. 'True to form, Jenner, you were late even for this simplest of tasks. I mean, what could be easier than waking up?'

'Mr. Henry, what's…what's going on? I…I can't move anything.' He struggled against his bonds.

'What's going on, Jenner, is that I'm going to teach you some valuable life lessons. If you live, you will be able to carry them on with you, thus becoming a better person for it.'

'I don't understand, Mr. Henry. Look, I…I promise I won't be late anymore.' He struggled against the straps again.

'Of course you won't, my dear boy. You're already here. I told you I was going to show you the ropes, I bet you didn't think I meant literally!' He laughed.

Jenner was terrified not being able to get a good look at his boss. He could hear the metallic clang of small tools being moved around, clanking on trays, being arranged, but could see nothing save the light bulb hanging by a cord above his head.

Henry stood over the gurney, looking down upon his charge. He reached up and tapped the bulb, its swinging cast shadows back and forth across his face, creating a truly sinister appearance from which Jenner could not take his gaze away.

'I've found that the moving light tends to burn these memories deeper into the cortex. Though I think you are going to have a difficult time forgetting this.' He clicked a pair of pliers in the air. 'Do you know what these are?'

Jenner's eyes were wide, his nostrils flared, his lips pulled back from his teeth. His mouth was dry as dust.

'I asked you a question,' Henry said, calmly enough.

'W-wrench?' Jenner's pupils had expanded, nearly covering the entire iris.

'I'll make sure to never put you on a maintenance detail. These are wire cutters.' The swinging light bulb illuminated Henry's face, changing his smile to a deep frown with every back stroke. 'We're going to start small, you and I. Would you rather I tell you what I'm going to do or just go ahead and do it? I'll give you that choice.'

'Please, Mr. Henry…'

'Very well; I'll tell you.' Henry lit a handheld torch and held it to the cutter blades. 'Must sterilize my equipment. Wouldn't want you dying from infection.'

'HELP! HELP ME!!' Jenner screamed.

Henry's smile quickly evaporated to a mask of lustful malice. He moved the torch close enough that Jenner could feel the blistering heat. 'Scream for your mother, little boy! Scream! Maybe I'll melt your fucking face right off. What do you think of that?' Henry laughed without a trace of humor. 'Now, quiet down so I can start your lessons. Do you hear me?'

Jenner nodded, silent tears fell from his eyes.

'That's better.' Henry put the torch down and wiped one of the tears away. 'See, you're already so thankful for what I am about to teach you that you're crying. That's a start.' There was a sizzle as Henry dipped the super-heated pliers into a bowl of water. 'That should be fine. Alright, let's get on with it. I'm going to start with your little toe, Jenner. You'll hardly miss it. I'm not going to lie though, this is going to hurt like hell.'

'Stop. Wait…please…my family…they have…' Jenner began to rock against his restraints.

'Yes, yes, struggle. It won't matter. Of course, it might affect my aim…we wouldn't want to lose an extra piggy, now would we?' Henry grabbed the little toe on Jenner's left foot and snapped it to the side, breaking it violently. He laid it flat against the side of Jenner's foot, watching the man's face for an appropriate reaction. He was not disappointed.

Jenner screamed loudly, spewing pop tart colored bile. He had never felt such pain. He didn't think it could get any worse—until it did. He felt a pinch, heard a crunch, and then ceased to register anything past the razor blades of agony that ripped through his skull. Henry held his dismembered toe under the swinging light of the bare bulb.

'Better close up that wound before you bleed out.'

Jenner could barely understand what was going on as Henry reignited the torch to cauterize the wound. He passed out cold when the smell of seared flesh reached his nose.

*

Jenner woke some hours later. Henry was there, standing over him, wiping the sweat from his forehead. When that was done, he helped the man to tilt his head towards a glass of water, which Jenner drank greedily.

'See, that wasn't so bad, was it?'

'Please, Mr. Henry. Please let...let me go.'

'I suppose I could, Jenner, but what have you learned?'

'I won't tell anyone!' Jenner pleaded.

'See,' Henry sighed. 'I don't think you're getting it quite yet.' There was another loud snapping and a cry of pain as Henry repeated the procedure on the small toe of Jenner's right foot. This time, it was many long minutes before his body allowed him to pass out. He was ashamed and sickened by the fact that the smell of his own charred flesh made drool form in his mouth.

*

'You look very pale, Jenner. Maybe this will help.' Henry pointed to a shelf on the far wall. A small light had been placed to illuminate two mason jars. Jenner's vision was blurred, and at first he didn't know what he was looking at. When the realization hit he screamed then wept aloud. His toes were lit up perfectly from behind, suspended in formaldehyde filled containers.

*

The next few days were a blur of disbelief and misery for Jenner. Terrified to fall asleep lest he lose another part, he struggled to stay awake through a mild narcotic haze. He developed oozing sores along his spine and around his groin, suffering unimaginable discomfort from not having moved in over a week. Despite his best efforts, he dozed fitfully through the constant pain. Snap. Clip. Had it been a nightmare? When he was finally roused from his stupor and allowed to sit up he focused across the room to the shelf. There were ten lit jars. Heart-wrenching sobs erupted from his chest as he looked down upon his ruined feet, ten blackened nubs where toes should have been.

'Eat, eat! He heard his torturer say. 'You're going to need to keep up your strength for your next lesson.'

Hunger cramps betrayed Jenner as he looked upon the heaping mounds of mashed potatoes, stew, and bread. He could not help himself as he ravenously downed the food.

'There, now. When you're done, you'll need to change your clothes. You've soiled them multiple times and I expect my employees to have a tidy appearance.'

'I can...you are letting me go now?' Jenner looked up from his food.

'Have you learned anything yet?'

Jenner studied the other man, sizing him up, keeping his face unreadable. Henry was older than him, but he was in a weakened state...and his balance...his breath caught in his throat as he imagined trying to stand...yet still...he had a knife and a fork. If he could get one lucky strike in, a stab through Henry's eye, perhaps, he might be able to extradite himself from this situation. He gripped the knife tight; adrenaline overcame his fear, forcing his burnt stumps upon the ground. The moment they took his weight, three of the wounds broke open, spurting a thick mixture of blood and pus onto the floor. He attempted to push off, but had no balance. He toppled over to the side, barely able to protect his head from cracking on the cold, filthy concrete.

'Ahhh. I see. I'm going to take that as a no,' Henry said as he helped the man back up onto the bed. 'I'd hoped by now we could have got you back into the rotation, though it appears you will never be a valet.' Jenner passed out as Henry's laughs echoed off the cold rock walls of the small, dark room.

Jenner startled awake. He did not know how long he'd been asleep. He could see nothing but a circle of dull illumination around him, a spotlighted specimen. He was once again restrained, a large needle fed into his arm from an IV bag hanging on a metal pole next to his bed.

'You didn't eat enough,' Henry said, tapping on the plastic tubing. 'And some of it came back up, I'm afraid. It does me no good if you die before I can teach you your lessons. Your very soul hangs in the balance.'

Jenner began to cry again. 'I am married. My...Paulina,' he sobbed, 'is pregnant with our child. I...I just wanted to send her some money so that she could join me here. Please. Mr. Henry. Let me go.'

'Where would you go, Jenner? Who would hire you now? Your chances of getting a job are severely limited at this point. No, your best bet is to stay here! Once your lesson is learned you will be an invaluable employee. This will be your home, a place to raise the child.'

'I have, Mr. Henry. I have learned my lesson. I will never be late again!'

Henry laughed and shook a finger at Jenner. 'You tried to stab me the last time you were unbound, Jenner. That doesn't ring true of what a trusted employee would do.'

Jenner strained against the thick belts and spat at Henry. 'Fuck you! You sadistic fuck! Let me go!' He lay back, exhausted.

'See? That's what I mean. You say one thing, and then do another. Actions are a much better indicator of where your true feelings lie. Tsk. Well, let's get to it. I'm a busy man; I've got a hotel to run, and I'm short staffed at the moment.'

Henry grabbed the pinkie finger on Jenner's left hand. He snapped it back like a dead twig. Bloody spittle flew from Jenner's raw throat as hoarse shrieking erupted from his lungs. Henry wiggled the broken digit back and forth until there was not much holding it in place except for the memory of the connection. He held the finger flat against the back of Jenner's hand as he grabbed his wire cutters.

'I suppose I should have asked whether you were a righty or a lefty before I did this, in case you are able to resume your duties.' There was a smooth slicing sound, like shears cutting a chicken thigh as Henry clipped through the tendon and muscle. He neatly removed the finger, holding it up into the light to get a better look. Jenner's eyes were rapidly rolling back into their sockets and closing as he saw Henry cross the room, spin open the lid to a fresh jar, and deposit the newly severed pinky inside.

Unlike his feet, Jenner noticed that Henry had neatly sewn the wound closed on his hand, when he awoke again.

'This can't be real,' he said aloud as he looked upon the macabre room. 'I've died and I am paying for my sins in hell. That's it, that has to be it. Please forgive me, Jesus; forgive me for all the wrongs I have committed.' Jenner more than expected a parting in the wall and a brightly lit figure to emerge, forgive him for all his sins, and whisk him away to a place of light and love where he would be whole again. When it didn't happen he thought perhaps he had not atoned sufficiently. He began to say the Lord's Prayer over and over until his throat became raw and voiceless.

'That's not the lesson,' Henry said as he entered the room unannounced. 'Words are meaningless; especially to God.'

Jenner continued his prayers gaining what volume he could. 'And forgive those who trespass against...'

His prayer stopped midway as Henry swiftly broke his ring finger at the knuckle. He then snapped it at the base. 'You said you were married; where's the ring? I guess we can add 'liar' to your dismal resume. I'm not even sure why I hired you to begin with,' Henry said with an amused lilt, as he cut off the finger. Over Jenner's screams, he spoke. 'Oh yes, I remember now. Because in Poland no one can hear you scream!' Henry started laughing uncontrollably. 'Oh my, I crack myself up! Did you get the reference?' He reached out and struck Jenner's face hard, the electric snap of fresh, brisk pain immediately awakened the man. 'I asked if you understood me!' Henry had grabbed Jenner's face and moved in close so they were nose to nose. He pressed as hard as he could, smashing the man's cheeks. Jenner could hear his jaw slide around in its socket as Henry squeezed harder. His lips and the insides of his mouth began to bleed as Henry pressed them into his teeth. Henry forced Jenner's head to nod.

Henry threw Jenner's head back to the cot and strode to the shelf where he placed the second digit into an empty jar. Then, suddenly calm and remote, he returned and meticulously stitched up the bloody void in Jenner's hand. 'I'll be back tomorrow to continue your erudition,' he said and yanked the chain on the bulb.

'Please...please just kill me,' Jenner cried to Henry's retreating form.

He turned back at the doorway, outlined by the dimly lighted staircase beyond. 'Kill you? Oh my heaven's no. I have no such intention. I'm not a murderer. I am an educator; the seeker of truth; there is no quicker way to get to knowledge or truth than through pain. Nothing strips off the veneer people wear like unbearable pain. Wouldn't you agree?' He looked long and hard at Jenner before he left the room. 'Perhaps we have not progressed enough.' He shut the door.

*

Snap. Cut. Jenner woke as dull pain entered his nightmares. His tongue was fat and dry; his speech slurred. 'You can't keep doing this...you'll eventually get caught,' he said as Henry entered the room hours or days later, it made no difference to him anymore.

'That's no concern of yours.' Henry began to whistle as he came closer.

Jenner screamed for all he was worth before the door could close. He had a surge of hope that perhaps someone had heard him as Henry raced back to the door, but instead of slamming it shut, he opened it wide.

'Go ahead, get it all out now!'

'I just want to go home,' Jenner sobbed.

'Home? *Home?!* This is your home. Welcome, here!'

*

Henry walked, whistling lightly, across the room to a small metal table near the ghastly shelves which now held over a dozen jars. He picked up a small silver hatchet, walked back to Jenner and examined the blade under the lightbulb.

'What's that? What...what are you doing? Wait...' Jenner begged.

'After ten toes and five fingers, you don't seem any further along. Perhaps you have become too accustomed to the cutters. One should not underestimate 'shock value.' Don't you agree?' Henry tossed the small axe up so that it flipped twice in the air before he deftly caught it by the handle.

'This is some sort of mistake, Mr. Henry... please...stop...please!'

'You are Jenner Greatine? Correct?'

'I am,' Jenner sobbed.

'Then nope. I definitely have the right person. Whew! Good thing we confirmed that.' Henry wiped his brow. 'Would have been hell trying to come back from that kind of mistake! I'd probably just have to kill you and hide your body at that point. Here.' Henry held a mouth guard at Jenner's face and was attempting to shove it into his mouth but Jenner was shaking his head violently back and forth in an effort to keep him from doing just that. 'I'm trying to save you some unnecessary suffering you intolerable fool. Would you rather bite your tongue off? You see, what's about to happen to you is going to be a....*special* type of event. I'm going to amputate that diseased hand from your body, hopefully keeping the infection from spreading to your heart—though I fear perhaps that is where the trouble originated.' Henry paused to ponder his words and then shrugged and abruptly started speaking again. 'No matter. Where was I? Oh yes...pain.'

Jenner winced at the mere mention.

'I wish I was better with the small axe, you'd think with all the practice I've had that I would be. But when I swing, as much as I would like to split your wrist perfectly between your arm and hand bones, I will inevitably miss to a small degree, burying the axe into bone. Now the good news is that I hone this blade to a razor sharpness so it will eventually go all the way through, but sometimes it can take a chop or two. Only once have I had to make three strikes.' Henry paused to consider the unintended pun, but went back to the business at hand. 'Now the problem is, if you don't wear the mouth guard you *will* break your teeth at the very least. The one thing about mouth pain is it just really never goes away, and your benefit package does not include dental. So I'll give you one last chance to put this in. I am chopping that hand off regardless. Your choice.' Henry held the piece out.

Jenner glared at him for a moment before opening his dry, quivering mouth. He gagged as the plastic forced his tongue back into his throat, but finally the guard settled into place and he closed his eyes.

'Splendid! I believe you have learned a valuable lesson…though there is a need to go on with our parameters set forth by the curriculum.'

Jenner mumbled a muffled plea and choked back sobs. 'F…fuck…off,' came quietly through his teeth before a mind numbing pain pushed out all thought of self. There was nothing save a red, savage, glare of torment.

'Can almost see the radiance of the Truth in that misery. Can't you?' Henry smiled, like a child looking for affirmation.

But Jenner's eyes had already rolled up into their sockets and he had passed back into nightmare and darkness.

*

'How are you feeling?' Jenner vaguely heard a concerned Henry ask.

Jenner realized that he was sitting up in a comfortable recliner and he was not restrained in any manner. Though he was drowsy, he felt slightly more clear headed. He twisted his bandaged arm to his face, attempting to wrap his mind around the fact that his hand was gone. He could feel it at the end of his wrist; he just couldn't see it there.

'Almost lost you. Wicked fever set in, I was fearful that Beelzebub was calling you back early before I had the opportunity to teach you your lesson.'

'Lesson?' Jenner was hoarse. 'All of this because I was late? Or was it...' he coughed, 'the shoes?'

Henry smiled at him, clasping his hands together. 'I hope you don't get angry, but I panicked when you were so close to the brink, so I...' Henry laughed nervously. 'Heh heh, I took your other hand off before you were able to pass over. I'm afraid that will affect your future employment.'

Jenner's face blanched as he pulled up his other arm. He stared blankly for two minutes, then tears began to leak from his eyes; soon they poured down his face. Henry coughed politely and turned away to give Jenner his privacy. He cried inconsolably for over a half an hour before he had no more tears to give.

Henry stood at his full height and faced his broken employee. 'Have you learned your lesson yet?'

'What are you talking about?' Jenner choked out.

Henry cocked his head to the side. 'You are a difficult pupil, Jenner. I truly thought...well, *I'd hoped* you were smarter than that. That's alright. There's still plenty more of you to take in penance.'

'Leave me the fuck alone you sadistic bastard! Just stay away!' Jenner swung a stumped arm at Henry missing by nearly a foot.

'Careful! You'll open up those sutures...you could suffer another infection.'

'Fuck you, you maniac! When I get out of here I'm telling the world what you did...what you are!'

'I do hope you tell them the whole story, Jenner, and not just your own, narrow view of it. I'll leave you alone, for now. You seem upset. But don't worry; you're well on the way to recovery.'

Jenner swung again but Henry was already half way out the door.

*

When Jenner woke this time he was once again restrained on the gurney. His eyes grew wide when he saw Henry again. This time, he had a bone saw.

'Don't even argue about this,' Henry said as he shoved the mouth guard in. 'It had been my hope to only take your foot but I've been...told that I have to take your lower leg from the knee down. You see I...well, since we have become so close, I will reveal a secret to you. I have a voice in my head. That's how I know truth from lies, where my higher knowledge springs. In any case, I learned early on that it's much wiser to heed what he says than to try and ignore his presence.'

Jenner was shaking his head back and forth, tears rolling down the sides of his face.

'I wish at least that you'd grasp the education here. I'm not a monster; I'm a teacher. This has become...unpleasant for me, I can't even begin to imagine how bad this is going to be for you. I have placed a tourniquet high up on your leg. Learned that mistake the first time I tried this. She bled out before I could even finish sawing through. Took me three days to get rid of that much blood, not to mention I'd had to hire another maid.... I have also added morphine to your nutrient drip. I am taking care of you, Jenner. I want you to come through this a better person. Right,' he clapped his hand over Jenner's knee. 'Let's get to it.' Henry pulled in a heavy breath. 'I've had to take on duties that you should be doing now, Mr. Jenner. Mrs. Crenshaw in three-twelve wants an extra bed in her room for her English Bulldog Hemi, and I aim to please. What a delightful lady...and that dog! If I wasn't so busy here I'd love to get one as a companion.'

The cords on Jenner's neck stuck out as he strained to move; his eyes bulged and a scream attempted to erupt around the rubber mouthpiece as Henry dragged those sharp saw teeth across the meniscus between the patella and tibia.

'At least this way I will mostly be able to avoid bone.' Henry leaned his forehead into his shoulder in an attempt to wipe away the sweat. 'Lot harder than it looks.' He smiled down on Jenner who had slipped quietly into shock, but Henry continued speaking anyway. 'This is tough work, but its righteous work. The Lord of Truth only asks of us what he believes we can give, and always for a higher purpose. And who am I to tell him differently?'

*

'I think you're starting to get the hang of this,' Henry said as he tilted Jenner's head up to allow him a drink of water. Jenner gingerly pressed the stumps of his arms against Henry's hands to make sure the other man did not pull the glass away. 'You were only asleep for two days. No fever, and I hope you appreciate the little bit of morphine; you seem much better.

Going to take you a while to get through the terror of all that you've gone through; it will haunt you to the end of days. I think they call it Post-Traumatic Stress Disorder. You can make it, though, especially with all you have learned. I can be a kindly boss once your education is complete. Your days of being a bell-hop are certainly over, though. Pity, but severe trespasses call for severe penalties. Am I right?' Henry stroked the side of Jenner's face in almost a paternal fashion.

Jenner wept, partly for the show of kindness, relief for the change in Henry's demeanor, but mostly for all he'd lost.

'Are you ready? I have others I need to attend to but until I've concluded my business here I can't move on. Just the nature of the beast.'

'Please…Mr. Henry, no more. I don't know what you want from me.'

Henry's head sagged. 'We've come so far, you and I; I thought by now we'd got past all that. I suppose not. I will allow you a couple of days to rethink your stance. You are much too weak for me to continue attempting to cut the cancer from you just now, but you will heal swiftly and we will proceed, if need be. I've brought some bread and pork chops—you should be able to squeeze them in between your arms. Please, Jenner, let's move past this. I'm starting to get bursitis in my shoulder from working with you.' For effect, Henry rolled his shoulder around a few times, before leaving.

Jenner looked at the now closed door. He was not restrained. He gauged the distance to the floor and the door and the hallway beyond, then perhaps…freedom.

'How am I going to do this?' he cried as he looked at the hard ground below him. He rolled off the bed and instinctively went to brace his fall with his non-existent hands. He'd not been prepared for the jolts of pain that rocketed up his arms and radiated out down his spine. It was many long minutes before he could even think to begin moving again. Blood began to seep through the heavy white gauze on his right hand, turning the covering a deep crimson. He had no way of propulsion that would not cause him unbearable pain; he did not think he could tolerate much more. He loathed the worm-like movements he made as he wriggled across the floor. When he looked up at the handle, all hope flooded from him. There was no way he could stand to get at it and even if he could, he did not believe he would have the strength or dexterity to grip and turn the latch. Eventually, he slithered his way back to the bed, then had no way to get back upon it. He spent two miserable days and nights on the floor hardly getting any sleep, pissing himself and weeping. He was almost begging for Henry to show up, he was so tired, hungry and dehydrated, though he knew it would mean more punishment.

'Tsk tsk, you tried to escape?' Henry asked as he came in.

'I did.' Jenner's head sagged.

'There's no escape, you should know that by now. What you've done has been done, no coming back from that.'

'No coming back from that,' Jenner echoed as Henry hefted his body back up to the bed.

'Well, I'm happy you've finally come to that conclusion, and impressed that you did not lie to me about attempting to get away. Have you had time to think?'

'I have, Mr. Henry.' Jenner had a glazed look to his expression.

'So I can put my bone saw away then?'

'I think you can, sir.'

'So then...tell me.' Henry pulled a chair up.

'She was so pretty, Mr. Henry, my Paulina.'

'She was eight, Jenner, and she was far from yours. She was your neighbor's daughter. Tell me, what happened?'

'I told her that Gertrude, that's my cat, had run away and could she...would she help me find her.'

'I am still amazed that in this day and age kids still fall for that one. Why is it that parents do not do a better job of teaching their children? Continue.'

'I took her into the woods...my pretty Paulina....' He stopped.

'You must continue, Jenner, that's part of this process.'

Jenner cleared his throat, a sob stuck in the crux; he took a moment to swallow and compose himself. 'I...I had my...my way with her.'

'Let's be clear, shall we? The time to mince words has passed. You raped an eight-year-old child. Is that correct?'

'Yes,' he cried.

'Then what?'

'There was so much blood, so much...she cried and I couldn't stop her. I choked her with these hands to shut her up...to make it all stop.' He held up his stumps, recognition dawning on his features as to why Henry had done what he had. 'Then I picked her up; she was so light, so...so fragile...the blood on her dress...I dumped her down the well behind my mother's house. Momma was so angry; I...I had to leave. I took the money from her purse and ran to the dock. I jumped on the first ship that would take me.' His head hung low.

'And are you sorry for what you've done?' Henry asked.

'More than I could ever express.'

'Do you know what happens now?'

'I have some idea.'

'You will have paid for all your sins once this is done, Jenner, you will start with a cleansed soul.' Henry stood and walked back to the door, he came back with a pair of garden shears.

'Will this hurt?' Jenner asked as Henry pulled the man's pants down.

'Undoubtedly, I'm afraid, but this is the pain you know you deserve to feel.' Henry gently moved Jenner's penis aside, placed his testicles in the vee of the shears, and in one deft movement, castrated the other man.

TWO MONTHS LATER

Jenner sat in a chair in the hotel lobby, a well-tailored, crisp blue uniform fitting his frame perfectly. 'On behalf of the Grande, it is an honor to welcome you back, Mrs. Crenshaw! How are you Hemi?' The dog's stumpy tail was wagging as it went over to say hello to Jenner.

'Henry has done much good here,' Mrs. Crenshaw smiled. 'But I do believe his finest piece of work is you, Jenner, dear.' She tucked a five dollar bill into his vest pocket and led Hemi to their usual room.

Part Seven

EPILOGUE

Matt Shaw

The vicar put the hotel manager's arm down and released his wrist. There was no pulse. The pale man's eyes were vacant and fixed on the ceiling and a morbid smile, as though he were pleased with himself, was etched on his face - frozen there by Death's cold grip.

Father Craig O'Dell looked towards the door and considered running, just as Tommy and Grace had done. He didn't need to be caught up with this either and the gun - still on the floor - didn't have his prints on it. It had *her* prints. She would be the one the police went after... But they would still want to ask him questions too. His name was on the booking form. He paused a moment - why was he panicking? Just because of his past - what did it matter that he was on the scene of another crime? He had been acquitted from the previous accusation. He was innocent. He was an innocent man caught up in another nasty situation and... That gun. It had her prints, not his. He could just call the cops and tell them what had happened... The girl had shot the hotel manager and - with the lad - had fled. He could explain how they had said that they had seen the hotel manager murder the other man in the foyer. Forensics... They could be able to determine whether that was the case and - if so - then... Well, the hotel manager and the dead man in the foyer would have taken the reason behind it to the grave with them. Whatever. Craig knew he had nothing to hide from this. Wrong place, wrong time...

'What happened?'

The voice came from behind Father O'Dell and caused him to jump. He turned to see Iain, another of the hotel's guests, coming down the stairs. His eyes had immediately fixed on the body by the door; the man with the slit throat.

'I don't know. I mean, apparently the hotel manager murdered that man over there and - then - he was shot by one of the guests who's gone and fled... To be honest... I'm as much in the dark as you are... I was just checking on the hotel manager but he's gone already.'

'Fucking hell... Called the cops?'

'Just about to.' Craig stepped over the body of the hotel manager and reached for the phone on the office desk. He lifted the receiver and dialled for the emergency services.

'This fucking city, man...' Iain shook his head as Craig explained the situation to the operator. 'No one ever realises how close they are to murder.'

THE END

With thanks to:

Wade H. Garrett,
Gary McMahon,
David Moody,
Wrath James White,
Kealan Patrick Burke,
Shane McKenzie,
Jeff Strand,
Ryan Harding,
Sam West,
Armand Rosamilia,
Mark Tufo
and Jasper Bark

Be sure to check out their work on Amazon!